MIST

THE PATH OF A KILLER

VOL. 1

JASON INSTRELL

The Book Guild Ltd

First published in Great Britain in 2017
The Book Guild Ltd
9 Priory Business Park
Wistow Road, Kibworth
Leicestershire, LE8 0RX
Freephone: 0800 999 2982
www.bookguild.co.uk
Email: info@bookguild.co.uk
Twitter: @bookguild

This work is entirely fictitious and bears no resemblance to any persons living or dead.

Typeset in Minion Pro

Printed and bound in the UK by TJ International, Padstow, Cornwall

ISBN 978 1911320 722

British Library Cataloguing in Publication Data.
A catalogue record for this book is available from the British Library.

MIX
Paper from
responsible sources
FSC® C013056

To the person inside us all, the inquisitive mind. The knowing and not knowing, but the ability to know more than others. To every moment in life that leaves its mark, to each smile and every tear. To wishing you had done more, to hope that you still can. To love the person that sticks with you, and to still love those that don't. To see beyond your normal perception.

To love life no matter what it throws at you, to forgive those that have done the throwing. To remind yourself you have a purpose, to remind others they do too.

To the life changing moments that shape our future, good or bad.

1

Dark; that's how I always know I've woken in the correct room – so dark; even with the faint glow of the morning sun shining through the small gap in the curtains, it still seems dark. The neighbour's property seems to lurch above my house casting a huge shadow that lingers straight over my bedroom. It's as if the dark itself were a person, gently trying to push its way into my mind.

John only had his left eye open. He squinted as if trying to see the most distant of shadows. He squinted just enough to recognise his dull, worn curtains hanging blissfully down the large wooden window frame. His other eye was fixed shut. As he began to focus he could see the light more clearly. He was fully dressed: shirt, black trousers and the shiny black shoes he hated so much and only wore on those special occasions. His left hand still held the whisky bottle, now warm to the touch, he had drunk from the night before. His right hand hung down the side of the bed just above the floor. He could feel the weight of his watch pulling at his wrist as if somehow trying to pull itself free from the mess it entwined. John took a deep breath – "Damn, what a night," he said to himself in a soft tone. Grunting with discomfort, he gently lifted himself off the sheets, the bed still made below him with the purple and gold cotton sheets his wife always insisted on. She said it was better for the skin... "God knows," said John to himself.

John sat on the edge of the bed. The alarm clock beside him

glowed a blue and green halo and the time, 6.45 am, seemed to jump out at him as he squinted harder adjusting both of his eyes. The lamp beside his bed still glowed faintly from the bulb under the cream shade. "Damn thing, fucking lamp!" John said. "Go off, will you!" John said again as he tapped at the base of the lamp trying to get the lamp to go off.

It was a touch lamp; not one of those lamps you could buy from any cheap market. This lamp was a high flyer; John's wife Claire insisted on it. She wanted the bedroom to have a boutique look as she put it, a soft and inviting environment... the sheets, the curtains and even the lamp all going with that theme. Not a man's room at all.

The sun lit up the room with a golden glow. It shone against the cotton sheets. Claire loved this room.

John sighed. "Well, another day, another dollar," he said, yawning widely. John put the empty whisky bottle down on the floor and gently loosened his wristwatch. The weight of the watch had left a mark on John's wrist that seemed to go deep into his skin. It looked pink and sore. John put the bottle and watch on the bedside table next to the lamp. Just as he did, the lamp came on again.

"Damn lamp. Why can't we just have a normal lamp? Fucking thing..." said John.

The light from the sun, now higher in the sky, began to push its way through the gap in the curtains. It pushed as if it had a force of its own, not letting anything or anyone in its way stop it. The ray of light shone on John's face as he sat on the edge of the bed contemplating how he got here and why he was fully dressed. The light was bright and forced John to shift position. John took a deep breath and rubbed his face. He could feel the stubble on his face tear at his hands.

John's room was quiet; as he sat on the edge of the bed gathering his thoughts, he could hear the faint noise of traffic outside. John lifted himself off the bed and walked over to the window. As he pulled back the curtains, the full light of the early morning sun rushed in. John closed his eyes for a moment taking the time to drink in the light. His right eye was still sensitive to the light. His room that once seemed so dark was now illuminated with the clean yellow glow of the sun, the warmth almost melting the Victorian glass pane as it passed into John's body. His white shirt, crumpled and stained, hung heavy on his shoulders.

John's bedroom window looked out on to the neighbouring house. It never used to be this way; the light would flood into the room but this soon changed when his new neighbours, Mr and Mrs Williams, built their all-singing-and-dancing glass extension. They had only been in the house a year and bought it from a lovely young couple; a teacher and a nurse John recalled. He liked them and they had been there over five years with no trouble at all.

John scratched his head and raised a half smile. The bedroom was the main reason John and Claire bought the property. The early morning sun and view over Leicester, plus the haze from the fumes that you could see sitting like a blanket over the city, made John feel at peace. It was crazy but John loved that scene. He liked the way that at night the light darted and danced on the horizon; he liked the hustle and bustle of city life. All taken away the moment Mr and Mrs Williams built that extension. John tried to stop it and had numerous talks with them, but to no avail. Something to do with 'Permitted development', John recalled, still standing at the window looking out at his once perfect view… *Never mind*, John thought, *times change*. John stretched his hands above his head linking his fingers and yawned deeply. His shirt lifted at the bottom exposing his hairy stomach.

2

John was thirty-nine years old, a tall, good-looking man, the type you saw in the movies with dark brown hair and a stocky build. He had a thin face, green eyes and a smile that could light up the day. He was healthier than most but didn't exercise. He was born in the East Midlands to a working-class family, his dad a carpenter and his mum a housewife. They lived on a typical street where all the houses seemed to sit together like a pack of cards, one gust of wind blowing hard at the first, and all the rest would follow. All the properties stood in line like soldiers on parade, the chimney pots sitting high against the blue skies. The drainpipes and guttering were all the same apart from sections that seemed to hang loose in areas. Not surprising, John always thought, due to their age. He was always amazed that the houses were left in this state, left until the water would almost have to flow through the bedroom windows before the owner would do something about it. On many occasions on a wet day you could hear the screams from number fifteen as the water hit the bed and covered Mrs Green. John would have loved to have been a fly on that wall!

The chimney pots were not used anymore as each house had its own gas fire, or electric glow fire in place just like John's grandma who lived four houses up. It was a glow fire that set light to the carpet in number twenty-five. John remembered the police cars and fire brigade as they burst into the house pulling Mrs

Franks to her safety. Mr Franks was not so lucky. The sirens and flashing lights lit up the quiet terrace street, all the neighbours out in dressing gowns and slippers, out like leaches crawling up a riverbank for fresh blood. Don't know what it is about humans but the slightest sound of sirens or flashing blue lights and they are out in the street like a shot. The fact that they never even knew the Franks, well didn't matter – when questioned they were best friends with them. John could still remember to this day the covered body of Mr Franks being carried out of the house. He remembered seeing the charred arm hanging loose down the side of the sheet, exposed to the light and being pushed on a silver trolley by two large ambulance drivers.

The look of pain in their faces said it all without even a word. The once blue protective gloves they wore, black with soot.

That image stayed with John for a while. John would see Mr Franks in his dreams, crying and weeping. The images clear and vibrant, John would hear every word Mr Franks said. He couldn't help it, as a child he didn't know what he was seeing.

The street went back to its normal settled self, as if it had swallowed an aspirin and taken a deep breath, and on doctor's orders, slept as advised. Number twenty-five was painted, cleaned and readied for sale. It was a routine of many landlords. The Franks' didn't own the property: they rented. The landlord was a large, fat man who drove an old Jaguar and smoked cigars. His shirt was always unbuttoned at the top and he smelt of stale whisky. He visited each month to collect his fee, six properties in total. The files indicated he bought these during the recession with money left to him in his mum's will. Jenny would always say, 'Look out, here is Two Jags!' He had two different cars and just to show his wealth, used different ones each month. He made your skin crawl, he had that way about him. John heard he died alone in a care home somewhere. No money, fuck all... pissed it on betting and beer according to people who knew him. What goes around comes around!

Workmen would come and go, filling skips with black, charred material. You could make out some bits: a carpet, a chair, but others were mere particles. The wind would pick them up and carry small bits into the air. The nearby cars were covered like ash from a volcano. George confronted them with this on numerous occasions, and John was sure his car was cleaned more than once as compensation. No one knew what happened to Mrs Franks after that. She wasn't seen again and no one talked about it. John did hear rumours that the 'bastard got what he deserved'! He didn't understand this at the time, but let it sit in his mind and dwell. He thought about Mrs Franks now and then, sitting in a cosy home with a garden, training and trimming her rose bushes.

John found out later in life that Mrs Franks (fifty-eight), had dementia and her husband Trevor (in his late sixties), wasn't coping. While his wife slept, which she did a lot during the day, he took some pills from the kitchen larder, opened the pot and swallowed them down all at once. They were sleeping pills according to reports, he took enough to knock out a horse.

Mr Franks was a stocky man, a builder by trade; not well liked as there were rumours he had murdered a woman when he was in his thirties. Apparently, he was having an affair with her and she threatened to tell Mrs Franks. No one knew the full story as no one came forward. Could have been gossip but these things hang around a person, like a dark rain cloud waiting to empty its deposits over a town.

Mrs Franks by all accounts had been a most attractive woman, but she couldn't have children.

The police report indicated he had taken twelve sleeping pills that day. The pill pot was found on the kitchen worktop, still in its place like a CD or video player that had been paused for that moment. The lid had been firmly placed back on and it sat just to the left of the kettle. A moment in time.

There wasn't much evidence from his body; the heat was

so intense it had cooked Trevor from the inside out. He could only be identified by his teeth. The SOCO photos showed this in detail. You had to have a good eye for detail to understand what you were looking at.

The fire wasn't raging, but what it did do, and you could think maybe deservingly, was light a section of rug which was lying half in the open fireplace, and half on the cobbled floor where Mrs Franks sat. An ember from this rug drew up the chimney breast and out into Trevor's room above. The rug didn't ignite further as the fire popped its fuse and cut out within minutes. There was plaster missing in the chimney breast in the bedroom above, plaster that should have been fixed long ago but like the guttering, sat open. This in turn exposed the smallest of cracks in the cement between the bricks, which allowed the chimney contents to spill into the room. The wind would blow through this and would whistle – it would cover the sound of Trevor's wife shouting and screaming in the other room from her night terrors. Sometimes the wind was so bad it sounded like the old kettles that people used to use. Trevor never got up and helped, but left her in her suffering. Even in the day he let her sit alone. His job was to be her carer. This is a strange word and can be taken many ways. In Trevor's case it meant he claimed the money, got her up in the morning, dressed her, washed her then left her sitting with the TV on. Washed her being a very over used word, her bed sores indicated this wasn't even completed correctly. Leaving Mrs Franks alone as he did allowed Trevor to roam freely, ignoring his wife's calls. Did anyone know she was treated this way? Maybe… but in those days, out of sight, out of mind! So, it was sheer luck that on this particular day, Trevor had moved his wife to the downstairs living room. She had her monthly visit from an NHS nurse for her check-up and Trevor always did his best to make sure she was presentable. It was Trevor's chance to shine as the caring husband! (Total bullshit!)

She wasn't his wife anymore; he hadn't felt anything in years since her dementia took hold, but he presented the scene well. They had no family so he was alone in his quest.

Trevor was a child abuser, the free time he had away from Mrs Franks allowed him to abuse his trust. He worked part time assisting disabled children at the local boy's club. Trevor would, on occasions, invite these children round his home. It was on certain days and only after the NHS nurse had been to assist his wife. No one thought anything of this as he was thought of highly by the club. He would lead them to the upstairs bedroom and abuse them. People were more trusting in those days and I suppose no one assumed anything like this would be happening.

He liked them round thirteen years of age. The abuse was so violent, both sexually and psychically, that the kids would have been scarred for life. The items he used were found in the remains. It was thought they were in the loft and fell through to the floor as the ceiling collapsed. Luck more than anything. Trevor took photos of his work, he did this on an old Polaroid One Step, the kind that develop the photo as you take the image. The boxes of photos were immense. The camera and photos were found in the downstairs larder. The images were disgusting to view.

The trauma and torment he caused these young boys was out of this world. Their disabilities just adding to the pain.

Did this cause Trevor to take the pills, to remove himself from his nightmare? No one will never know. Was he caught? Threatened. Blackmailed? All guesses. All the children were identified and the officers spent years concluding the case. Many of them couldn't remember the incidents, shut it from their minds. The mental disabilities they had, assisted them to forget.

What was known was that Trevor didn't suffer. By the time the ember met his bed sheet, and set fire to the quilt that covered Trevor's body, he was already gone. The fire worked quick and fast. It ravished the room and was so hot it stripped the paint. All six layers of colours painted year after year. John supposed he got what he deserved (*I would have liked to have hanged him,* John would think) or did he take the easy way out...? What was for sure was the abuse stopped at number twenty-five and Mrs Franks survived the fire.

What was also made clear was the part Mrs Franks played in his death. Mrs Franks sat downstairs with her tray in front of her carrying a small glass of milk. The milk was warm from the sun beating through the living room window. The tray was on wheels and was made to pull in front of your legs and place itself at eating height. This had been pulled to her so tight that her blanket, that was once covering her legs, was hanging loose at her feet.

The tray had a paper, which was four days old; an apple, bizarre because she couldn't eat or drink herself; and a small box of tissues. The police report indicated she was neglected. The scene backed this information.

What was clear is Mrs Franks started the fire.

As she sat in her single chair, bolt upright, the blanket covering her feet, the tray lurching straight over her lap and the sun beating in her face, Mrs Franks pushed the electric fire with her right foot. The police think she was trying to move the blanket off her feet. She pushed it so hard that the electric glow fire, which was right near her feet, tiped on its face.

After only what would have been a minuite, the rug set on fire.

It was as if she had known what to do, and with her new-found strength took the moment by the hand and acted.

No one will ever know for sure but John liked to think that, for that moment, she was the Mrs Franks Trevor had married, and the one who put a stop to his evil ways. The Mrs Franks that came back to this world for that moment and took the law into her own hands and ended the monster's work.

9

The rug was large and old, covered in dust from years of not cleaning, the thick tassels on the end bent and twisted. It was one of these tassels that wrapped itself round the electric element, dislodged with the heat… and was sucked up the chimney by the vacuum to Trevor's room. The element of the fire could have touched the other section of rug below Mrs Franks' feet, but it didn't. She survived. The fuse blew just before anything else took hold and the fire cooled down. Call it fate or call it what you will. John called it justice! He heard she was smiling as she was wheeled from the house. A neighbour had seen the flames and called the services, and he had broken the door, which was locked (strange, as it was never locked), and rescued Mrs Franks. She was carried outside slung over the neighbour's shoulder, her night gown rolled up, and one slipper missing. It was a sight straight out of a comedy film. John was told only a year ago, she spent the rest of her days in a rest home up in the woods and she passed two years later from her illness. She had the time to see the outdoors, and experience just a bit of life before the disease fully took hold. She was fully cared for and the nurses loved her. She was never left alone again, and spent the rest of her days with people that cared. John did see a photo of her with the staff at the beach in Weybourne, he was sure she was also smilling!

3

John was a good student but had trouble concentrating. As he got older this settled, the doctors made sure of that. The nightmares would come and go and John would wake up out of breath. It was as if his chest had been crushed by some unknown force. He would dream of falling through a tunnel that was spinning all around him, shapes passing him by. He always struggled to make these out but he knew they were not good. John would run downstairs crying and it would take several minutes for his mum to calm him down. She would sit John on the kitchen worktop, give him some honey and rub his back. This always calmed him and allowed his young lungs to suck in the fresh air he needed. She made the honey seem magic. The smell of tobacco from the living room would give John a sense of calm, although hurt his eyes if he got too close.

John's dad, George, was a stocky man. He would sit in the same chair at the same time most nights, the papers strewn across his knee and the TV blaring out with the six o'clock news. John always wondered what his mum saw in him. He always wondered if it was love at first sight, or if it was one of those chance meetings. Who knew…? The only thing John knew was this was his father and it wasn't what John wanted to be. He was a hard man, too hard to be with a woman such as Jenny. She was a beam of sunshine. She lit up every room she entered, her presence seeming to lighten the darkest rooms and she could always bring a room to attention with her warm laugh. John loved his mum. It wasn't John's mum that pushed him to take the medication, it was George.

'I'm sick of that bleeding kid,' he would shout, as if trying to get the attention of someone outside the room but knowing that they were close. 'Why can't he be like his brother?' he would say. This always upset Jenny; she didn't show it but looking back John recalled how she hid the tears and pretended something was in her eyes. George smoked roll-ups. He had a small tobacco tin he would open and pick at the contents. Each piece inside the tin was laid out neatly. The rolls he had made sat one by one. Twelve in total, John recalled. The pride in his eyes as he made these small items come to life.

He could also remember George counting them several times, checking and turning them as if making sure one hadn't been taken.

The morning and evening routines of George were intense.

He would sit in the same chair, his big yellow-stained fingers would fiddle and roll the tobacco, and he was so concentrated that Jenny's questions or shouts washed over him like a shower. John remembered the smell to this day. John had never smoked. The smoke that bellowed from them was potent, not like normal cigarettes, a lot more stronger and darker smoke. The yellow walls were only apparent when you lifted a picture from its nail; the clean, bright paint or paper below would appear to you, the stained, tarred walls around you darkened by years of cigarette smoke. Why Jenny stayed with him no one knew. He didn't earn much and just made enough to keep the family's heads above water. John thought this made him feel like he should be treated as a god… or above everyone else in the family. Without him they were nothing… who knew?

John had a brother. He was two years older than John, he was stocky after his dad and seemed to have inherited the same attitude to life as George had. John remembered he wasn't in much. John would be in his room reading or watching crime drama on his small fifteen-inch TV, while Mark would be out playing football. It was a hot summer that year. There was a lake near to where they lived, surrounded by woods. The trees seemed to curve round the perimeter of the lake as if protecting its very presence. In summer, you could stand on top of the creek, look down at the lake, and the reflection of the sky and sun was breathtaking. It almost seemed like heaven. John would sit up there on warm days, legs crossed, pen and paper in hand, and draw whatever took his imagination. John was six at the time and his brother was eight.

That summer was a particularly hot one; it was the summer holidays at school and both John and Mark were at home. The living room was lit by the warm sun rays as they passed through the glass into the room. The silver and bronze fire half glistened in the sun. If you looked at it too long it almost burnt your eyes, the floral wallpaper on the walls picking up small flints of light as it formed rainbow colours over the space. Jenny loved the light.

The faint jingle could be heard from the wind blowing the chimes in Jenny's backyard. It wasn't a garden but a small backyard. Jenny always called it her garden and had done her best to plant the space bringing life and movement to a dull grey area.

The wall adjoining John's house and the neighbour's was thick with beans. Jenny grew these in a small patch of dirt no wider than a spade. She grew them to shade the wall.

John and Mark had great fun in the summer break barging in and out of these beans, although George didn't approve. The beans would bang and drop to the floor. John was always amazed at the length they grew and how this tiny soft package could house such tender items. John always saw the world differently to his brother and Jenny loved this in him. How the beans and pots of plants grew as they did, John never knew. Jenny had an art of taking the worst-looking objects, and with her care and attention they would blossom. The sun was limited to a few hours in the morning but when it lifted and settled to its final position in the sky at midday, the garden dropped into shade. George loved this as the light affected his eyes and also stopped him watching the TV which was perched in front of the window. He hardly moved from this space. John was sure he only saw him move to use the bathroom, that was it. George insisted John and Mark went and played. George worked from around 8 am until 5 pm. John knew when he was on his way down the street as he could hear the rumbling of the Chrysler alpine engine as it screamed and guzzled through the fuel. If he was in, he made haste. He never knew what mood his dad would be in. George had that effect on people.

Playing out in those days was safer; the boys could play for hours outside, disappear on their bikes without anyone raising an eyebrow. Mark did this often. They were surrounded by parks and green areas. In the summer these were full with kids from different areas, all ages. It looked like a bees' nest on the park near John's house, thick with kids packed on every part of grass. Hustling and bustling. If you looked from high above, you would think it was the largest bees' nest you'd ever seen.

John and Mark loved the park. You would never see an adult unless they were walking a dog and you never heard abuse or anger; just the noise of the football and the distant train rolling by, and the birds flapping in the branches as the balls hit the tree posts. It was a good time to be young. There was a large acorn tree with long twisted branches in one corner. It hung low and the weight of its branches seemed to pull it closer to the floor.

John loved to climb this tree.

He would climb all the way to the top. He liked the feel of the branches swaying in the wind, the breeze blowing blissfully against his face.

It made him feel free. Jenny would see him now and again and nearly collapse with fear at the sight.

On Monday, 20th August, John's brother, Mark, vanished at the age of eight. George and Jenny lost their oldest son. Mark was a strong swimmer, always had been, but something changed down at the lake. John spent his time sitting on a broken tree trunk swinging his legs up and down. No one knew how the tree trunk got there, or why it sat on Pebble Beach as it is known, but it did. The trunk was hollow inside and if you were small enough you could squeeze down the inside. The small pebble area near the edge of the lake wasn't much of a beach; more a bank, a bank where the marks of the night animals could still be seen the morning after. The feathers from some unsuspecting bird lay clean on the ground. Dots of blood lay over them. John drew this as he sat on the log. He studied it intently, he thought deeply about the situation. He looked in detail at how this creature had come to meet its end. He always, even at a young age, had a mind of intelligence. He stripped back the scene in his mind… just as he had watched on TV. He sat looking around him for the smallest detail. He could see the small marks in the pebbles, scratch marks, John thought at the time, and he could see the blood splats on the pebbles, but there was no body. John assumed this was a large animal, maybe a fox. Even at his young age he couldn't understand why a bird would be caught by a fox.

He knew birds moved fast and he knew if a fox crept up on the bird from the brush, its movements could be heard and the bird would flee. He knew the scene felt wrong but drew it as he saw it. He looked around at the tall pine trees and listened. You could hear the faint bird song; you could hear the far sound of a siren going off in the background. He tapped his pen against his pad, thinking deeply.

Mark was flapping and jumping up and down in the lake. His top, shorts and small shoes lay on Pebble Beach. He had

15

on his small swimming trunks that seemed tight against his big frame. He swam round close to the shore; the water was very cold even in the summer. The large trees towering over the edge of the lake seemed to keep the light from passing to the edges. You could see the centre of the lake glistening in the morning sun, although this was much too far to swim out to. It was 10 am but warm. Mark was jumping and trying to catch the small fish that swam in and out his legs as he stood in the cold water.

John knew the exact time as he always wore his small watch, although his brother laughed at him; he liked to keep track of time. Mark would make large splashes, which would jump John from his concentration.

The only way to the lake was through a man-made path that led through the woods. It was made of wood and seemed to be built on stilts off the wooded floor. It swerved its way through like a large python avoiding the big trees and smaller obstacles. It had a purpose, a purpose leading to an end. The lake. Some of its boards were loose, the years of neglect taking their toll. You had to step over the gaping holes just to make sure you didn't slip through into the marshy land below. The green algae from the damp woods covered the deck. When you walked, your footprints seemed to lift the green algae leaving clean wood below. The marsh below the path was dark and wet, you didn't know how deep this was so you made sure you watched your step.

You could fall in this and go so deep, no one would ever find you. This thought always stuck in the kids minds in those days. Made you aware of what you were doing.

For years, the lake had been a nature reserve, open to the public, but protected. Over the years this had dropped off; neglect, lack of funding, always the same old, same old... At night, it became a dark place used by local drug users and drunks. How they negotiated their way over the broken path was amazing, would have loved to have seen that! At the end of the path the lake was fenced off and large brambles grew against it forming a wall of brambles that almost acted like barbed wire. The sign 'Keep out, private property' was fixed at numerous intervals. There was a small gap in the fence that only a child could fit through, John and Mark squeezed through this. It didn't get many visitors in the day anymore, the kids mainly spending their days on computers at home. John and Mark didn't have this so had to amuse themselves. Mark's normal batch of friends was at a party; it was a ninth birthday party for Sarah. Sarah was a local girl who was in Mark's year at school. He had a crush on her and avoided her as much as he could. The other kids knew this and taunted Mark.

He had made a card at school and managed to slip this in Sarah's bag. He hoped she had this and looked forward to seeing her at school after the break. Mark wasn't as good at school as John; you could say Mark was a tearaway. John on the other hand was a good student.

It was 1 pm when John left the beach and went out of the fence into the woods for a wee. When he came back, Mark was gone. No noise, no marks, nothing.

It was as if the lake had swallowed him up in one, taking every part of him; his shoes, his shirt and his very existence. Nothing was left on Pebble Beach. The environment looked clean and tidy. The scene that had met John and Mark on their arrival, and had taken John's attention, had gone. The peace was almost deathly, the splashing water had stopped and a stillness had found its way to the water.

The sun still lit the centre and the pattern of the trees could be seen on the bank. To John, at that moment, they felt like towering soldiers. A shiver came over him. John shouted and shouted but nothing.

He knew Mark liked to prank, and was sure he had gone back home seizing his chance while John wasn't there. John stood, his hands to his mouth, shouting loudly… nothing. John looked around, surveying the scene. He picked up his notebook from under the log where he left it, and looked round for his pen. The pen was gone. John put the notebook under his arm and fled back through the wood.

No body or evidence was ever found to indicate anything that day. No blood or traces. There was a vast search for Mark, the weeks flew by. It was on the news and all over the radio. They used the family name in the paper as if to strengthen the story:

'Public mystified as young boy disappears in a Mist!' John remembered at the time how cruel this actually was, but he was used to it having a last name of such fun; although they always dropped the 'e' off the end! The police search was vast, no one came forward... John was the only witness to this. They searched the lake and the woods and found nothing. They even searched the marsh, the best they could with the depth. John told them everything he saw and heard. It was filmed but due to his age, proved difficult for the police. The bird, the blood, the bent barbed wire fence, the smell of burning wood John picked up as he leant against the tree. He told them everything. John watched the film later in life. He watched this young boy in front of him speaking so clearly and clutching his notebook. The detail that his young mind remembered.

The questioning officer gently asked point after point but as softly as he could so he didn't rattle the child. This was DCI Vickers, a tough bastard... Why they let him speak to kids was beyond John. He had one of those faces that looked like worn leather; wrinkles from ear to ear. And when he concentrated more, the wrinkles joined up making him look like almost a mouth with no eyes. He was a hard bastard... no time for bullshit. He died of lung cancer at the age of eighty-eight.

Mark Miste was now a cold case and sat in the police archives gathering dust. It sat with the numerous other unknown cases, evidence still wrapped in bags gathering dust. The dark cellar with moving bookcases, a place to behold. If they could talk… Jesus! Mark's file sat on row 4, shelf 2, next to a file of another missing boy.

John's notebook was in the file, along with his statement.

John went down from time to time and looked over the detail… hell, perhaps one day something would make sense! Nothing!

The Bible – *forgive those who trespass against you* – easier said than done; you have to know them first!

A few things happened after this: 1. George didn't speak to John ever the same again as he blamed him for the loss of Mark. He continued to smoke but more heavily. 2. John went on some yellow-looking pills to stop the dreams and visions he was having. This started two weeks after Mark's disappearance. 3. Mark was never found.

The beans in the garden stopped growing, the light seemed to fade in Jenny's eyes. She did get this back but it wasn't the same. The loss of a child can never be described in words. It's a pain that only a mother can endure. John would hear the arguments at night echoing through the walls; the questions, the 'why us?' and 'where could he be…?'; George slamming the door as he headed out to drink leaving Jenny with her thoughts. Quiet…

Jenny passed away when John was twenty two and was still in his training with the Police force. She was so proud of John. She passed with breast cancer, but she held on until John graduated. She hung on until John went to the hospital and showed her his medal, certificate and graduation report. George even managed to lift a smile as he sat at the side of her bed playing and banging the TV remote. The words 'well done, kid' squeezed from his dry lips. It had always amazed John how a person's character stayed with them even at the worst of times.

'Always remember Mark,' were her final words to John. She passed one night later from complications. Her words had stuck with him all his life. Even when he dreamt of her she said the same thing. George died several years later from a blood clot. He married again, some bit of skirt he met from down the local club, but John never got involved.

She moved in with George at the house, she shared his home and his life and they went away several times. She was a widow and lost her husband in a freak accident at work, although she was paid out greatly by the insurance, as John recalled. They both suited each other, both like magpies filling their nests with gold, both single-minded in their approach. John supposed the situation suited them both, more company than anything. George had his waitress back and Mavis a partner. George left the house to Mavis, and on her death John was meant to inherit it. Mavis passed away a few years later having squandered all her savings (£500,000). She was knee-deep in debt and had secured loans against the house. After the funeral and debt costs, John received a cheque for £1,650.45… don't forget the 45p; most important! To this day, it still sat in a bank account. John left it there as a reminder of the most important thing in George's life, Money!

John graduated top of his class. He had a gift for detection, a gift that stayed with him through his career.

4

John stood in front of his window, his eyes both focused now on the light seeping in. He had pulled the curtains all the way back as if inviting the sun in just that bit more. He could see the extension next door glistening and sparkling as the sun filled the room. *Typical* John thought. He unbuttoned his white shirt, took it off and threw it on his bed... trousers and shoes followed. The room was now filled with light, the rainbow colours seemed to dart around the room, the particles bouncing off John's chest and falling gently on the floor. The whisky bottle on the side shone in the sun. John looked at this and thought... *What a night, what a night...*

John made his way out of the bedroom and into the hall. The Victorian semi had high ceilings and seemed to have hundreds of doors. It was a Victorian three-bed property, nothing special, your typical layout with two rooms and kitchen downstairs, with three bedrooms and a bathroom upstairs. The house was quiet. The pictures on the walls were the only indication of life outside these walls. Photos of John and Claire as happy as could be, were strung up on the walls. The pictures were in straight lines, not one out of place. John liked this... symmetry... he couldn't stand anything out of its place. "Bloody things," John said as he levelled up the end picture, the picture that seemed to move with every door slam or movement on the corridor. The one that balances on its nail and jumps off at you the moment

21

you walk by. The corridor wasn't long, just long enough to take all the doors. The ceilings were high and in the middle was a loft hatch covered in stained glass, the roof light in the loft above lit the stained glass throwing a pattern of colours on the walls and stairs. It wasn't dark like the bedroom.

John went into the bathroom and stood in front of the sink, looking at himself in the mirror.

"God… never again… too old for this sort of thing…" John said as he patted his face to make sure he was really alive and this wasn't one of his elaborate dreams.

"You're never too old, John," said a soft, faint voice from the hall. "Thirty-nine… Handsome stallion…"

"You would say that," John said raising a smile as his hands rubbed either side of his face now covered with stubble from the late night before.

The reflection back seemed to age more with every look and glare. John opened the mirror-fronted cabinet and grabbed his toothbrush. The blue one with two stripes, not the pink one; that was Claire's. Beside the toothbrushes, was a small tablet container on which were the words 'John Miste, anti-depressants'. The rest of the writing was gibberish to John, lots of that doctor crap and terminology they spoke. He was sure they only said these things to make themselves feel bigger than the person in the seat opposite. He had listened to this more times than he cared to remember… the monthly sessions… *same old, same old*, John thought as he picked up his blue toothbrush.

"Supposed to stop sensitivity," John proclaimed. "My arse… Doesn't help me at all," John said again, as the toothbrush pressed deep into his mouth. He turned the tap on taking the brush and wetting it as he continued. The toothpaste on the brush smiled up at him. The crystal-clear water ran into the cast white sink, and the drain took the coloured water away stained with the toothpaste that fell off the brush.

John brushed his teeth, put the brush back into the holder in the glass cabinet exactly as it sat previously. He turned the brush several times with his right hand until he was happy it was in the right position, counting in his mind *One, two, three, four, five, six... That will do*, he thought.

John combed his hair using a brush he seemed to have had for a long time. John had dark brown hair, fairly long. People said movie-star hair. But John liked it that way. He combed and combed until it showed some sign of order.

Just at that moment, his mobile rang...

"It's in here, John," said the faint voice from outside in the corridor.

"Where?" said John.

"The living room," said the voice back.

John rushed out of the bathroom and made his way down the stairs. His legs felt weak from the night before so he thought he must have danced the hell out of them. He grabbed hold of the oak banister and made his way down. The rays of coloured light bounced off John's back as he descended

"I'm coming... I'm coming... damn phone... wait a minute..." said John as if the phone itself was a person, waiting to take orders and obey as told.

"DI Miste," John answered.

"You sound out of breath, sir," said the voice on the other end.

"I've just ran down the bleeding stairs I'll have you know, and I'm not dressed!" said John with a hint of sarcasm in his voice.

"Thanks for that image, sir, that will stick with me all day now.

It's 8 am, sir, we need your attendance urgently... A murder, sir, very messy."

"Okay, okay, spare me the details until I've put some clothes on," said John. "I'll meet you all in the briefing room," John said then hung up the phone. He placed the phone on the kitchen worktop. He hated the things. He just about remembered pagers but knew technology was there to stay and in most ways, it made life easier. Google… email… Facebook… it was all still a mind-fuck for John.

The call was from DS Walker, John's right-hand man, or to be politically correct, right-hand woman. John had got in trouble with this before. She had worked with him now for six months, although it felt longer. John didn't keep partners long as he was known as being weird at the station. The one who 'muttered to himself'.

John could hear the chatter in the police canteen, he could hear the quiet whispering when he walked in. It was as if speaking in a quieter tone made them less apparent. For detectives, John thought, they were foolish. They all sounded like small muttering mice fighting for a piece of cheese.

5

John opened the fridge door; the light illuminated the kitchen. The warm glow glared out at John, still in his underpants but with perfectly combed hair. John lifted a bottle of milk from the fridge, took the cap off and gave it a good sniff. He knew the smell tickling at his nostrils was good. The pure white liquid gently danced inside the clear crystal bottle. He put the milk to his mouth and took a long, good drink, the gulps of fresh milk running down his throat cooling as they went. His sore throat from the night before was screaming for more to take away the taste of beer. His tonsils almost danced as the crisp cool milk passed them by. He heard once from a friend that if you drank a pint of milk after you'd been drinking it made you sober!

Bullshit, thought John. *Makes you feel sick*, he thought as he drank from the glass milk bottle.

"Take it easy, John," said the soft voice.

"I know… I know, I know you hate it," John said with the milk bottle pressing up against his forehead, the cool bottle cooling his weary mind. John leant on the fridge with his eyes closed taking in the milk's cool taste and even cooler feel. He took long, deep breaths. Images of him and Claire danced through John's mind, boxes that seemed to open and close and each time they did, a new image appeared.

"I remember that time," John said in a laughing tone with his eyes closed and milk bottle still pressed against his head. "God, it was fucking great," John said again.

The light in the fridge flickered as if trying to get John's attention and invite him to close the door. In the silence, the compressor in the fridge gently kicked into life. John opened his eyes and slowly brought himself back to the current moment. He took the milk bottle from his head, which was now cool and had on it signs of water from the bottle. John placed the half-drunk milk bottle back in the fridge. He placed the milk cap back on. He took the milk cap and placed it on and off several times until it settled in the correct position so John was happy with it.

"Third shelf to the right," John said out loud as he sat the milk on the shelf of the fridge door. "I think a fridge says a lot about a man... don't you, Claire?" John said again in a soft tone.

John pushed the fridge door closed. The fridge was a retro-looking unit; it was cream and shiny and matched the kitchen cupboards; very modern, sleek and new. John and Claire had this fitted out only a year ago. It was their Christmas present to each other. At the time, John wasn't sure about the look, but Claire soon calmed his doubts in the way she always did.

"Ten thousand for a damn kitchen, ten thousand? Shit," John said, standing with his back to the fridge and looking round the kitchen.

The blind in the kitchen was open but the kitchen didn't get much light as the neighbour's extension had made sure of that.

"Bastards... should have been bright as hell in here... Typical; no thought for anyone else," John said whilst looking out at the large glass monster next door, the Berlin Wall as he put it, climbing high and casting the biggest of shadows over their garden.

John walked to the window and looked out into the garden. The empty pots and containers said it all. The dead climber trying to cling for life against the old brick pillars. The garden was small, but a tranquil place. Its walled look was what Claire loved; it made her feel safe and sound. John and Claire saved for a long time to get this place. It was typical of a Victorian semi.

"Open the front curtains, John, let the light in," said a faint voice.

John looked round from the kitchen window and standing so clear was Claire. She was a small, petite girl, with a figure John loved. Curves in all the right places John would say. She was wearing her bed trousers, the ones with cats all over them. John never knew the significance of this but it made him smile. Her top was bright yellow, clinging to her petite frame. Her dark brown hair hung each side of her head, long – at least to the middle of her back; her face and radiant smile, her soft and caring blue eyes.

John took in the scene, a soft, caring smile on his face. He leant against the sink as if taking in a masterpiece or portrait in a museum. The peace and quiet around him was sensual, the faint sound of a bird could be heard in the background singing its morning song. John's eyes were wide open, the image in front of him was breathtaking. His heart was at a steady beat.

"You'll be late for work," Claire said. "You need to get dressed and get moving... you'll be late," she said again in a soft tone with a smile on her face. She had her hands on her hips. John knew this pose as she did it often; the pose of authority, the pose of you're right and I'm wrong. He got to love this over the ten years they had been together.

"Okay... okay, I'm going, I'm going."

John walked towards Claire into the living room. Claire stepped aside to let him pass, the smile still bright on John's face. His hair sat neatly on his head, his bare feet gently tapping against the tiled floor. The living room was dark so John headed straight to the large Victorian window and pulled the blinds. He opened them full mast. The early morning light flooded in the window, the large Victorian panes of glass drinking in every section of sunlight. The lines of light filled the room and the dust particles could be seen flying and darting around.

"There, that's better. Are you happy now?" John said.

"Much better. Shame about the mess," Claire said pointing at the table.

John had left a stack of magazines on the table, empty glasses and a plate that seemed to have something growing on it that resembled the dead climber outside. For such a clean man, John wasn't that bothered about the front room. He spent most of his time in the spare bedroom, or study as he called it, on his computer. The front room for John was a walk-through only.

"Yes, yes... nag, nag... I'll sort it later," John proclaimed as he looked round at Claire now sitting in the armchair patting the dust frantically with her left arm.

The particles raised into the air and glowed against the sun's rays as they met.

John left Claire sitting in the armchair and headed upstairs. Time was getting on as it was 8.30 am now. He headed to the master bedroom, opened the large wooden wardrobe and grabbed his clothes. John rarely wore suits, he didn't believe in them. He thought it made him look like an undertaker or a banker... he stuck to civilian clothes as he put it, far to the dislike of his superiors. John checked his hair and face again then headed back downstairs. On the stairs sat his keys and ID cards. John grabbed these and put them in his right pocket. He wore jeans. They were not tight but baggy and they had deep pockets which John liked. He liked how he could hide numerous things in there. A Tardis, he called them. John picked up his small black notebook and pen, an idea he stole from the old crime programmes he used to watch and it stuck with him. These went into his left pocket. His wallet pressed in his back pocket with the change bloating it out.

"Damn milk is coming back up," John said rubbing his belly. "Load of shit that drink, milk, rubbish," John said again.

"I'll see you later," John said turning and looking at the armchair.

Claire was gone… no noise, no sound. The house was silent. The sun shone through the Victorian window lighting up every space now. John looked frantically round the space standing with his back to the door, stretching his neck like a swan. He had his hands on his hips. The front door opened straight into the living room. It had a large panel of glass in it with coloured lenses. The red and green patterns glowed against John's blue shirt. The halo of light pricked at his hair.

Claire was gone…

"She must be at work… or upstairs… or perhaps…" John stopped at that point as the door behind him let out a large 'Ding dong', the noise of an old-fashioned church bell. It was on the door when John and Claire moved in and they stuck with it.

They thought it matched the Victorian splendour.

It rang again, this time making John jump and step out of his trance.

"Yes, yes… one minute."

John pushed his shirt into his jeans and straightened himself up, his neck still craning around the room. His eyes narrowed with concentration and his right hand was up against his face rubbing against the stubble. He looked intently into the room studying every angle with his detective mind, looking for clues of Claire's release. *When…? Where…? How…?* he thought.

The bell rang again behind him…

"Yes…" John said in an angry tone whilst swinging open the front door. "Fuck sake, Wren… fuck sake," John said.

"You look flustered, sir," said DS Walker… or 'Wren' as John and the team liked to call her.

"You made me jump… I was… well, I was… It doesn't matter," John said still fiddling with his collar, buttoning and unbuttoning his shirt.

29

"Right, okay, sir… right… ahh… sorry about that… Are you ready to roll?" Wren said.

"Yes, yes, I'm ready, I'm ready," John said in an angry manner. "Let's get moving."

"I thought it was quicker to pick you up, sir, with the traffic and all that," said Wren. "We need to head straight to the scene as forensics are moving fast," said Wren again.

"Yes… yes… okay… let's roll," said John still fiddling with his shirt collar.

Wren was a good cop. She didn't leave school with any qualifications and didn't have a good upbringing from what John could gather. But she was a good cop. She was in care from the age of ten when her parents split up, then pushed around the system for years, never knowing what bed she would be in the following year.

Everyone around her thought she was a bad egg but Wren could read.

If there was one thing she did on those dark nights alone in foreign beds, was read. It kept her mind occupied and allowed her to shut off the noise and crap around her.

She fell into police training accidentally; it was more 'you only have a few options, Miss Walker'… That old chestnut.

She chose police. It suited her and she slowly made her way up the ranks. She had a nose for bullshit and John liked that. Her peers noted behaviour issues as she grew older but the force put this down to her situation, and for this reason, drugs were not needed.

6

She was placed with John at the Leicester branch of CID six months back. John's old partner, Glen, or Grey as they all called him, had retired the night before. He had been on leave after being attacked and stabbed several times whilst chasing an assailant. It was touch and go for a long time and he was in critical care. His wife and two daughters were by his side. John got on with them although he couldn't do the dinner and chat thing. Grey was a stocky guy and when he ran at you he was considered an elephant. *Couldn't run for shit*, John remembered, *but a tough guy*. He didn't stand a chance: they were both on a case and John apprehended an assailant on the ground floor, as Grey approached the door upstairs and opened it slowly, he was attacked. Grey was stabbed several times in his back. How the hell he didn't die, John didn't know. Doctors said his sheer size cushioned the blow.

Shit... never seen so much blood... and I've seen some shit, John thought.

The party for Grey was good. The police hired a room above an Indian restaurant in town, just down from the railway station. A quaint little place with only three windows. You had to walk into the restaurant door off the street, wave a waitress who would come gracefully over carrying a menu, then try to explain you didn't need a table but you were part of the private function. John spent ten minutes trying to persuade her. She didn't speak

31

very good English so when John said, 'I'm with the police', it may have thrown her out… Managers, bar staff and the guests in the restaurant all stood to attention. Jesus, you would have thought Elvis had walked in. It was lucky Wren walked in when she did as John was beginning to get flustered, his face red and his brow watering from the heat of the suit. Wren walked in dressed in casual clothes, not as John was used to seeing her. She flashed her invite and the waitress nodded in approval, and she pulled John with her to the small stairs to the left. John still looked at the waitress in bewilderment. The function room was large and you would never have thought that it would open out this big from the small dark stairs that met you, and the single door at the top lit by a large fluorescent hanging loose on a wire, but it did.

The room was spinning with disco lights and the music was banging.

As John walked in fully suited with Wren by his side, the others clapped and laughed including Grey. They all wore casual clothes, some even in shorts, while John was suited and booted even with a tie and his shiny shoes.

"Bastards… you bastards… I should have known." Grey always knew how to have the last laugh. John's invite was made slightly different to the rest; it was edited and changed in such a way that John was told it was a dinner party. He did think it was strange in its location but didn't think to question Grey. The photo of John in his suit, look of shock in his eyes, was sure to appear somewhere in the office, they always do! John would see the funny side, although no one would ever admit putting it there. It was amazing in all the gloom and crap around you how small things could change the mood. Even if it was for everyone else's amusement, it would make John's team smile.

John saved Grey's life with his quick thinking. He chained his assailant to the large cast-iron radiator downstairs and ran upstairs on hearing his partner scream. He had his CS gas and small baton, and though the attacker was gone, John grabbed

32

Grey and pulled him to safety, dragging him by his arms from the room as quick as he could while surveying all around him. Grey's body was limp and lifeless. The blood was pouring from him. The puncture wounds could be seen as clear as day on his back. The office talks about John carrying Grey all the way to the hospital… They spoke like John was a hero. 'Shit… if I was a hero he wouldn't have been stabbed,' he would say. Still, made a change from the normal mutterings. Grey understood John; he put up with John's mutterings and speaking to shadows – they were together eight years. That's a long time in the force.

I'll miss the bastard, John would think.

Wren walked John to the car. It was a black Audi, one of those compact ones; John wasn't sure as he wasn't good with the modern-day vehicles. Wren had slung the car into the first space she saw, which to John's frustration was further up the road than he would have liked.

The Victorian street was packed with vehicles, bumper to bumper like books stacked on a shelf. All different makes and models.

The street was tree-lined – John and Claire liked this. The street was Abbey Street.

It was a typical street of Victorian semis that lined Leicestershire's main roads. Urban but quiet.

"Shit, Wren… couldn't you have parked further away?" John said in a joking fashion.

"Sorry, sir… next time I'll call in collection and have the car lifted from in front of your house and mine lifted in," Wren said in her joking manner.

Watching Wren and John walk down the street together was a strange thing: John; tall, handsome, casually dressed, his thick brown hair gently moving from side to side, six-foot in height but thin. Wren; short with a bit of weight on her, black hair slung to one side, she always wore a long black coat even in summer that hung neatly to her feet. Sparse make-up as she didn't believe in it. From the back it looked like she was floating and had no feet at all. It always looked like a scene from *The Addams Family*. John took this as if he was Lurch... this made him smile. Suppose they both went together as they were both, in their own way, different.

Wren's phone rang as they got to the car.

"DS Walker," Wren said. "Yes... yep... I will... right way..." said Wren again to the caller. "We need to go straight to the scene, sir. Very messy, very messy they tell me."

"Give me the low-down," John said as they got to the car door.

Wren pressed her key but the doors didn't open. She pressed frantically at the button. Wren never swore; she used other fitting words to John's amusement.

"Bugger... bugger... what's up with this again? Been meaning to get this fixed..."

"Bring back the good old key locks," said John.

Eventually, the car doors burst into life and the indicators flashed as if to say, ' OK, we give up, we just wanted to see you both stand their a while longer!'

"Thank God for that," John said. "You can feel the curtains twitching," John said again.

They both got into the car. It's neat and tidy presence pleased John. Wren always kept a clean car. The car freshener hanging in the window with a big smiley yellow face and the words 'Please visit again' on the back, told John it was washed on the weekend, and by the garage on the main road as they were the only ones who handed out that particular brand of car freshener.

"Shit, I've left my phone... shit... Too late now; they will have to call you," John said to Wren patting his jeans and trying to recall his steps.

"I left it in the kitchen. That's you rushing me!" John said in a raised tone.

34

"Oh yes, Chief said to tell you, answer your phone!" Wren said with a faint smile on her face.

John laughed at this. Wren was good at lightening the mood.

Wren pulled out of the space and headed up the road. The crisp Monday morning sun was shining at the window. It was a fine spring morning: cool breeze but nice. John liked spring although the low sun always made him squint. John pulled his sunglasses from Wren's glovebox, placed them on and sat back in the seat. They lived there all the time as John didn't drive. He had a licence but took the bus. He found it less stressful and it gave him more time to think and work. The time was 9.25 am.

It was then that it hit him…

Fuck… fuck… fuck… my pills… John said in his mind. He put his hands to his face and covered his eyes.

He remembered the small glass pill bottle with his 'happy pills' as he put it sat neatly in the bathroom cabinet. He was going to take them but got distracted.

He knew it had been three days now since he had taken them. He also knew that without them, the images, the voices, the sense of pain polluted John's mind. They gripped and teased at him.

"Do you want to stop off at the cemetery," Wren said in a soft voice.

"What…?" said John half breaking his mood.

"The cemetery; it's the next turn," said Wren again.

This broke John from his inner thoughts, it grabbed at his mind and dragged him kicking and screaming back into the car. He lowered his hands from his face. Wren had hit a nerve. It was not a nerve that made you twitch or jump, like when you banged your funny bone; it was a nerve that made you stop dead in your tracks and stare into space, thinking about a situation before you acted…

"It's Claire's birthday today, isn't it?" said Wren. No reply from John.

"Do you want me to stop off?" said Wren again.

"No," said John in a quiet but strong voice. "No… no need, thank you…" John said. His eyes fixed at the front window; not even a blink, just a glazed stare.

The red lights turned to green and the Mini in front of Wren's Audi pulled off in a screech. The traffic was heavy. On the left was the cemetery opening, its large, imposing black gates standing proud against the crisp blue sky. The willows and silver birch blew gently in the breeze. The large brick walls constructed with blood and tears by the builders, stood tall. It was three miles from John's house. John looked at this as they drove by, and the time seemed to slow to a standstill.

John looked out of the door window with his face fixed at the cemetery gates, a tear settled in his eyes. The sense of peace was on his face. As the willows blew and gently rocked, so did John's thoughts. Backwards and forwards in his mind. It was like a roller coaster of emotion: you were up then you were down… black… silent… pain… memories all hitting at once like a machine gun firing several rounds.

I love you, Claire, John said in his mind. *I love you*. John blinked and closed his eyes. For that moment, he was at peace.

7

Claire was murdered in November 2014, the year before. It had been hard for John as she was the love of his life. John was working on a case, a real shit, deep case. It involved a serial killer that the force named the Wolf. They called him the Wolf because of the way he left his victims. He would stalk them for weeks; take his time, no rush. He would gather the most in-depth information on them. Schools, family, likes, dislikes. He would then befriend them on Facebook. He never met them from what John could gather and no one ever saw his face. No family, nothing. He was invisible. The Wolf would attack. His first victim was a young girl of sixteen; her name was Lilly. The Wolf had worked on her for a few months, the evidence showing from the Facebook accounts, and her diary, were that they communicated regularly. Nothing sexual, just chit-chat. Lilly was walking home over Braunstone Park at 5 pm. She'd left her friend's house just the other side of the park. She had done this walk many times before. It was November and cold, slight rain but nothing heavy. The ground was wet. She never made it home. It was 6 pm when Lilly's mum, Mary, called it in. Lilly's head and left arm were found in the brook just left of the path. The area is well lit and the houses look over the brook. The body parts were placed in the water, the position made it look like the body was somehow under the water swimming in its depths as the head was the right way up, and the arm was under the water but visable. It took thought and time to place the body this way, a real mind fuck! it was a strange sight to behold. It played tricks with your mind. The mist covering the brook made it worse, it looked like an old horror film. The brook wasn't deep. Lilly's small face was neat and tidy and no signs of struggle could be seen. It was as if she fell asleep that way. No footprints, no blood, no clothes, no noise… nothing. No prints on the wet bank. SOCO scoped for hours but found no trace. The Wolf came in, took his prey, and disappeared into the night. It was thought he walked the full brook to remove any chance of footprints. Still to this day it's incredible as it passes through several villages with numerous points of access. Someone somewhere had to see. Nothing! How he could have walked this distance in water was beyond everyone! There were prints traced at the far end of the brook, over 1 mile from Lilly's body, they were boot prints but consistent with numerous walkers in the space as the area was woody and marshy.

There were over one thousand prints just in that area. If he left at that point, the Wolf knew what he was doing.

This was the first of fifteen victims John worked on. Always different body parts found, never a full torso. Claire was number fifteen.

The only prints and evidence found at her murder, were hers.

Last year Claire had been at work as normal; it was a Wednesday. She was a teacher at a primary school not far from where John lived, a quaint little school called Imperial Avenue. She had worked there for five years and had already made her claim to the position. She loved children and although they didn't have a child of their own, John knew someday soon they would. Claire walked to school and back as it kept her fit and if the weather was bad she took her small bike that she had had for years. She would wear a black and white raincoat far too big for her frame. It hung down way past her knees. How she peddled with this, God only knows. Claire loved that bike. The damn thing clogged the hall at home and on numerous occasions was known to fling itself at John as he walked in. It was Wednesday 10th November, a normal day. Claire kissed John goodbye at home and told him to remember to put the bins out as it was bin day… 'Don't mix up the recycling,' she would always say. How John could mix it up was beyond him as it was different coloured bins, but he amused her and said Yes, honey.' Claire left home at 7.30 am on the dot. Nothing different, nothing of any significance. John left at 8 am when Wren arrived outside.

According to the school she didn't arrive at work.

At 9 am John was called by Mrs Grange who was the head of the school and a good friend of Claire's. She had in fact been round to John's on several occasions for coffee and a chat; 'coffee and a chat', a woman's thing, not John's cup of tea. He always made himself scarce. She was a key player in bringing Claire to the school. Claire was poached from an infant school the other side of the city and Imperial gave her the chance to teach the age range she loved. She did it so well. At 9 am when she called John, he was sitting at his desk, a pile of paperwork standing tall against his computer.

The pile was so high John had to stand to see Wren and engage in any conversation. The Wolf case took a great deal of time. The reports, files, cross-checking… John was a stickler for detail and checked things again and again. The Wolf case was one of two he was working on at this time. John answered the phone to Mrs Grange who had asked how Claire was as she hadn't turned up, but John knew she had left as he had been at home that day and saw her leave.

John had been desperate in his tracing. Turning every stone he could, his superiors wanted him off the case but he stuck hard. He was the only one who knew her well. At 1 am on Thursday morning the following week, a barman called Ben pushed open the back door to the bar where he worked. He held two bags in his hands, waste and food. He walked into the dark alley only illuminated by the faint yellow light glowing near the back door, the normal flicker of a bulb well past its prime. The door was metal in structure and painted black to blend in with the tall dark walls. It was heavy and always took some force to push. It was painted this way so it didn't look like a door and blended in. Ben always got the task of taking out the rubbish. There was no CCTV in the alley; no need for it as the towering bar walls and the neighbouring property formed a tunnel, dark and quiet, leading to a dead end. The alley wasn't long, but always felt cold and imposing at night. The odd drug user or drunk could sometimes be found slumped in one corner. If you stood and looked hard enough in the sky, you could see the faint light of the stars. The bins were directly in front of young Ben as he walked over. The bar kept these locked as the alley was open to the main street. They had had issues with vagrancy in the past, and the bins being opened and the rubbish strewn over the street. The council had warned them more than once, forcing them to lock them both. As Ben approached he noticed the blue large bin was unlocked. These were not normal bins you had at home, these were the large industrial bins on wheels. You had to get up close to the bin to even notice the locks, such was the darkness of the space.

The bins were the type you see the early-morning bin men wrestling with through the city centre, and even on the odd occasion, you could spot one rolling off as if trying to escape with its contents, two bin men running after them at full speed. John saw this a few times and even had to stop once to assist. Ben placed the bags on the floor in front of him and lifted the bin lid. The faint light from near the bar door glowed yellow and dull, the faint flicker from it making flashes of light bounce off the bin's paint. You could only just about see the bins to fill them with waste.

The police were not sure if it was the smell or the sight that made Ben faint, but the sight that confronted Ben wasn't what he expected.

Claire was found bound and gagged, her naked, petite body lying in the bin. She lay between bags of waste; she looked as though she had been carefully placed. Her hands and feet were missing; cut clean, the pathology report indicated. The bin had been filled many times after she was placed as it was readying for its weekly collection, its sheer luck (or bad luck) that Ben spotted her when he did. A bag had moved off of Claire's face exposing her white complextion, the smell adding to the scene. It looked as if the Wolf had planned for her to be collected by the bin men, and taken to the tip, where she would have disappeared forever. If it wasn't for the bag moving off her face, she would have been lost. Perhaps this would have been the best solution for John.

Reports indicated that her limbs were cut while she was alive. She suffered. The cuts were so clean the reports said that a mechanical cut, or a spinning blade was the most likely cause. The type of blade that cuts clean through the largest of trees. The small spurts of oil, and indication of grease on the wound, sealed this conclusion. She was not cut at the scene as there was no blood present near the bins. Only blood spurts in the bin itself. The decay had set in and it wasn't a nice sight to behold. She was starved and dehydrated, her once pretty complexion gaunt and removed. The flies had started their work at the bare exposed bone and tissue.

The South Leicestershire branch dealt with the call; it was sheer chance, or divine intervention, that John wasn't on that shift. He was only called once the body was identified.

Her face was calm with no sign of struggle; it was as if she just fell asleep. It wasn't until the autopsy that the note was found. A note was placed in Claire's mouth. It was rolled and tied. It was placed within a small food bag, and sat on Claire's tongue. The jaw was then closed tight. This could have been lost, with the body, if Ben hadn't found her. It makes the Wolf seem an even sicker bastard as you can't be sure if he wanted her found or not!

The note was to John.

DI Miste,

Can you hear it, John? Fate, it's fate that binds us, and it's fate that keeps us together. The mist surrounding you, John, the pain and the suffering, the voices, John. I know all about you. I've watched you, John. I know your moves before you do. What do you see when you're alone and the demons come? I see Little Red Riding Hood trying to escape the Wolf's clutches. I see pain in your eyes, John. Happy hunting, John... happy hunting.

John read the note and identified the body. It was without doubt one of the worst things John had ever had to do. The loss of his brother, his mum or even the Franks were nothing compared to this. To lose a loved one, a person you share your body and soul with... there were no words to describe. John took sick leave and returned four weeks later. The other deaths had been bad, the case had run John's life for a long time, but this... nothing compared to this.

The pills helped and the visions of Claire and his conversations with her helped ease the pain. To John she wasn't gone, she was there, clear as day. *The doctors... bastards... can say what they want... she didn't die... she is as close to me now as ever!*

The Wolf's note remained folded in John's pocket. It was supposed to go into evidence, but to this day John still had it. No fingerprints or evidence were pulled from the paper. The Wolf was too careful for that; he knew the systems and processes, he knew how to cover his tracks. No prints were taken from the scene, he was careful and clever.

8

John and Wren pulled up at a park, just outside the city. It was called Watermead… God know's why, but it was. You had to pass under a large yellow height restraint to get to the car park. This was to stop the site being overrun by caravans or lorry drivers parking at will. The Watermead sign stood large and proud. It was on a large metal stand beside the park opening. Graffiti was drawn straight over the edge of it and the word 'tossers' in bold black ink. The overflowing bins were placed strategically round the site, the putrid smell of them clinging in the air. It almost tickled your tonsils as you breathed. There were large concrete barriers placed evenly either side of the barrier. You could walk through or bike through but cars wouldn't stand a chance. The car park could fit around thirty cars at a push. The large police vans and vehicles were clogging up the area.

As John and Wren pulled up, a sergeant in full police uniform approached them. Wren wound down the window.

"DI Miste and DS Walker," said Wren, showing her badge which she kept in a pink wallet rather than the police issue. Every time she dragged this from her right pocket it amused John.

"Sergeant, I hope you guys haven't pissed on the evidence, elephant feet as normal, and can we please seal of the area?' said John.

"No, sir, no one has moved until you got here, as ordered…

sir. The area is sealed, we have officers at all park entrances, sir," said the sergeant with a faint hint of worry.

John shook his head.

The sergeant stepped back from the car and waved John and Wren in. John leaned back in his seat, settling his head back down on his shoulders. Wren placed the ID card back in her pocket and gently moved the Audi onto the car park.

The gravel clunked and cracked against the tyres. The sun shone almost blindingly at the front window of the car, so badly that Wren leant forward clutching the wheel tightly. She clutched it as if she was on a racetrack and everything was at stake. John looked over at her clutching the wheel with her tongue placed firmly between her teeth; the concentration was immense. He smiled. He took his sunglasses off and folded them neatly. John folded them several times, in and out before placing them back into Wren's glovebox. His sunglasses always sat tidy in Wren's glove box. Wren watched John's ticks in full force.

"I see the ticks are still at play," said Wren.

"Ticks? said John.

"You know, the counting thing…" Wren said again but indicating with her eyes and head movements towards the glovebox where John had just placed his sunglasses.

"I don't have ticks," said John.

"Ahh yes, we call them comfort thoughts. Was that right?" Wren said, still concentrating on the path ahead with the sun blinding her as she gently rolled forward.

"Can we not talk about it please? We are here to work," said John in a blank manner.

"Talk about what?" Wren said looking at John with a raised smile.

John looked at her and smiled. "You're a pain in the arse, Wren… a pain!"

In her rear-view window she could see the sergeant take off his hat and wipe his brow. John has this effect on people.

People would say it was an authority thing, but Wren knew it was his knowledge and demeanour. They didn't know how to handle John; with what he had been through he should have cracked but he didn't. This made him somewhat powerful to his colleagues. Like a cat with nine lives.

John was DI of the serious crime unit. They operated this with a small, dedicated team, a team John had worked with for many years. They were all there when Claire's life was taken. South Leicester worked on the case with John and his team assisting. John's connection making it very sensitive for the force. John didn't like the pussyfooting around him, how even the whisperers were trying to be nice. Still... it soon faded away. Funny what time could do.

Wren managed to park the Audi in an immaculate position in the car park. It was parked perfectly in line with the police cars; you would have thought it had been there hours. There was a sharp bank in front of the cars that shaded the rest of the park from the car park. John rubbed his face. It had taken nearly an hour, and John's mind had been racing the whole time. Not having his pills was not a good thing. He managed just about to keep the images at bay, but without his pills they piled in. His doctor asked him to describe it once... what he sees.

'It's like someone has turned on a TV, but unlike when you watch TV you concentrate on one programme, this one in my head flicks between images. Sometimes so fast it hurts...' John told him.

The doctor asked if the images were known, and John said yes. 'People I've lost, cases I've worked on, same bullshit, different day.' It was always put down to stress from the things he had seen in life, even as a young boy; same shit. John always wondered, if he stretched his case file out, he bet it would reach Birmingham... he thought how many megabytes of data he had used up on the doctor's system. It hurt his mind to even think about it.

"Coffee?" Wren said.

"Where the hell did you pull that one from then? We are sat in a park car park… and don't tell me it's that shit coffee from the SOCO van!" John said in a joking manner.

Wren pulled a silver flask from behind her driver's seat. Her small arms could just about reach round at the back. She had to unbuckle her belt to get some leverage.

"There you go, made fresh this morning by my fair hands, sir."

"You never cease to amaze me, Wren," John said, looking at the shiny silver flask sat on Wren's knee, glowing so brightly with the sun from the windscreen, John had to narrow his eyes.

9

The time was 10.05 am, the traffic had been bad and had held them up. The scene that stood in front of them was panic: there were suited police officers; there was the SOCO team. All of them were very busy. Blue gloves and blue shoes on. This was the police base camp.

John opened Wren's flask and started pouring coffee into the flask cup. It was always coffee in this flask! He took a sip of the hot coffee, lightly sugared. Wren watched and smiled. Wren was still pulling at the handbrake; it was stiff and awkward to use.

"I'll do it," said John with a mouth half full of coffee burning at his throat.

John put the flask cup down, wiped at his mouth and with both hands pulled at the handbrake.

"There... don't want us coming back to a car in the bleeding road, do we!" said John with a soft tone.

"Thanks, sir, what would I do without you?" Wren replied.

John and Wren stepped out of the car, John still with the flask cup in his hand and the sun made him squint deeply. Wren stepped out of the driver's side slamming the door as she left.

"Bugger... bugger set, damn you..." Wren said to the car key.

With a flash of the indicators, it set.

"DI Miste, I presume?" a voice said behind John as he stood, coffee in hand, surveying the car park.

"That's me, and this is DS Walker," John said, pointing at Wren with his free hand. John wasn't wearing a coat, although there was a chill in the air.

"Really messy this one, sir, really messy!" proclaimed the officer.

The park was in the south of Leicester, a different region to John's force. John already knew this the moment he pulled up. He also knew that if he had been called, there had to be some sort of connection. The SOCO tent had been built over a small area to the side of the car park, standing between two of the bins and slightly in shade of the hill that stood proud in front of them. John surveyed the area and noticed two cameras, one either side of the car park. They stood tall on the poles that towered high.

"I want footage from those two cameras sending over to me ASAP," John said to Wren.

"The car park; any indication of a vehicle or signs of struggle?" John said to the officer.

"No, sir, forensics gave us the all clear to set up here this morning," said the officer.

"Who is she?" John said.

John pointed to a woman using his free hand while still grasping the hot flask cup. She was sitting with the typical police issue red blanket wrapped round her shoulders, slumped in the back seat of a marked police car. Her legs were hanging out and placed on the gravel. She wore running shoes that looked brand new. Her hair was brown and tied back in a ponytail and her hands were clasped round a paper cup, the steam from the hot contents rising in front of her face.

"That's Sophie Jones, she lives local, nice girl..." said the officer.

"Wren, go over and have a chat, see what she knows," said John.

"Yes, sir," said Wren.

Wren left John standing near the car. John hadn't moved far but was taking in the scene, his eyes darting around every corner of the car park, his mind drinking in every detail. He took slow, steady sips of his coffee. John kicked at the gravel under his feet. The park entrance was at the end of a long crescent. It was a dead end and the houses finished back in the distance. The park entrance was a blind spot and was out of site for the residents. The rows of semi-detached houses lined both sides of the crescent as it winded down.

As John and Wren drove in, you could almost feel the curtains twitching. The area was deprived, a council estate that had seen better days. *Makes sense with the graffiti and rubbish,* John thought. The street lamps stood either side of the street with the last one finishing to the right of the park entrance. A pair of old trainers, gently swinging in the breeze, had been lashed over the telephone lines.

Fucking shithole, John thought as he let out a shiver. John had his right hand to his head, shading his eyes. He didn't wear sunglasses out of the car as he found it disrespectful. The beer from the night before was now a distant memory, although every now and then he could taste the milk he had gulped before he left home.

Wren called over to John.

"Sir," said Wren, waving her hand and prompting John to walk over. John took one more sip of his coffee and put the flask cup on the roof of the Audi. He stood it perfectly in the middle so it didn't slip off. He fiddled with his shirt as if tidying himself for court and fumbled in his pocket for his ID. The gravel crunched under John's feet as he walked over.

"This is Miss Jones, sir. She was running at 7 am this morning, her normal route, and spotted the victim. She called it in at 7.30 am," said Wren, reading from the notes she had just taken. John had a good manner with people although he was imposing. Claire used to say he had an aura about him, whatever

49

that meant. Sophie was sitting, her legs still trembling from the shock earlier. The blanket was pulled tight and the cup lay between her feet.

"Not very nice, luv, is it?" said John to Sophie, showing her his ID card.

"Pardon?" she said looking up at John with a frowned expression thinking he meant the picture on his ID!

"The tea," John said pointing at the cup lying on the floor, and the puddle of tea seeping deep into the gravel.

John flapped his ID card shut and placing it quickly back in his pocket.

"Oh… ahhh… no… no, it's not," said Sophie, looking puzzled. Wren was also looking at John as bewildered as Sophie was.

"I never drink it, Miss Jones. We bring our own; it's safer," John said with a smile.

He said it loud enough for the officer near the police van to turn his nose at John. The police took the "tea" van with them if a site was to be a long haul; normally called in and asked for by the DCI.

John had a way of rubbing people up the wrong way, but it was the way he did things.

John had a smile on his face and still had his hands covering his eyes, the sun belting down on his head and his hair was damp to the touch.

"You don't look like a police officer," said Sophie.

John smiled.

"I'm DI Miste of the serious crime unit," John said. "I don't like those uniforms as they make my skin itch," John said again with a raised smile. Sophie raised a smile still, shaking from the experience but starting to settle in her environment. John knelt in front of Sophie; he liked to get to people's level…

"I've never found one that actually fits either," John said. Sophie raised another smile.

"Do you like running, Miss Jones?" John said, looking down at Sophie's trainers.

"Call me Sophie," she replied, staring at John's head with a miffed look as he continued to look down at her trainers and didn't look her in the face. Wren was still standing with her notepad and pen; she stood listening contently.

"I used to run... back in the day; used to swear by it, loved the freedom... then work took over. Never seem to get the time now. I used to run around our local park, counting the laps," John said, shrugging his shoulders but still looking down at Sophie's trainers.

The scene around them was getting busy. It seemed like hundreds of officers were beginning to surround the area, controlling ever aspect. There were people standing behind the police line staring at the scene in front of them, and at the tent covering the crime scene.

"Sir, I'll go and speak to Jacob," said Wren walking towards the tent and leaving John kneeling down near Sophie.

Sophie looked at the gathering crowds and let out a shiver...

"They wouldn't stand gawping if they saw what I saw..." she said.

Sophie had a common voice; she was an attractive girl with brown hair and a good body. Her hair was tied back but you could tell it was long. She was petite but had something about her. On her wrist was a small gold chain. It had the words 'I love you' on it as clear as day. She was fit looking, but John thought, not running fit.

"Are you from round here, Sophie?" John said lifting himself up from the ground and patting down his knee where he had knelt. The small bits of dry gravel dropped to the ground taking Sophie's attention.

"I told the other lot, I live at the top of the road at number six. I have a partner and have one child," she said in a raised voice and with a tone that suggested she had been asked this several times previously.

John nodded and looked round at the scene, he pulled at his trousers and tucked in his shirt, he put both hands in his pockets and gave a nod.

"She is lying," a voice said.

John smiled to himself and without knowing said, "I know… I know," out loud.

"Pardon?" said Sophie. "Are you talking to me?" she said again with a tone.

John ignored her question…

"Your trainers, Sophie; your trainers confuse me," John said again.

"What?" said Sophie.

"You were out running, you came across the victim at 7 am, then called it in thirty minutes later. Is that correct?" said John standing in front of her with his body covering the sun's glare against Sophie's face. Sophie was taking in John's words and trying to think carefully what she was hearing. John's eyes looked her directly in the face. He looked as if he was reading the pages of a book.

"That's correct. Why… why do you ask? I've already told the other woman the same as I've told you. Why do you ask me the same again?

And what's the problem with my trainers?" Sophie riggled in her seat and pulled tight at the blanket round her shoulders.

Just at that point, Wren appeared back with John. She had left the tent.

"Sir, you need to come over, forensics need to see you," said Wren, looking deeply at John's face.

John took some gum from his pocket and gently opened the silver wrapper; he placed the gum in his mouth and began to chew. Wren and Sophie looked at him.

"I'm sorry, did you want some?" said John, aiming the gum at them both. No one answered. His eyes were still fixed to Sophie's trainers.

John started to walk away from Sophie and followed Wren to the tent, the gravel crunching under both their feet.

"Excuse me… excuse me, what were you talking about a minute ago??" said Sophie. She had lifted herself up from the seat and stood clear as day near the police car, the red police blanket still hanging round her shoulders and her neck stretched out.

"What?" said John stopping and turning, chewing vigorously at the gum. "Don't let me drink again, Wren, will you?" John said to Wren quietly.

"No fear of that, sir, you'll never live it down after that suit performance. Or the dad dancing," said Wren in a similar, quiet tone.

"What…? Dancing? Explains my legs… Was it…?" John's conversation was interrupted…

"My trainers," Sophie said again breaking John's chit-chat with Wren.

"Ahh… yes," said John. "That's right… your trainers, your trainers…"

John turned and walked back over to Sophie until he was stood in front of her, a warming smile on his face and his sense of presence. Wren stayed exactly where she was surveying the scene.

"Your trainers, Miss Jones," John dropped the 'Sophie' and became formal, "they are too clean for a runner. Too clean… not a splash of dirt. Yet you say you ran from number six? That's half a mile up the road," said John. "It would have taken you say ten minutes to get to this scene; that's as a confident runner," John said again. "We passed it, DS Walker, on our way in, you remember?" John said, again turning and looking at Wren. Wren nodded gently with a sense of knowing. "That road is dirty and is wet from the night's rain, the paths are stained. If you ran, I would have expected some splashes and dirt, at least on those trainers," John said again. "Even a patch of dirt on your

53

legs?" John chewed at the gum and turned to walk away. Sophie was looking stunned and silent. She was looking down at her trainers, looking deeply at them. You could sense her brain whirling around, the cogs and switches taking in what she had just heard.

"So, Miss Jones, I would say you were walking either from home or back to home. The trainers are too clean for someone who has just run and then there is your make-up! Why would a runner wear full make-up?"

John knew running; he had run several marathons in his time and John and Claire had completed the London Marathon twice. Claire never wore make-up as she wanted her skin to breathe. It made her sweat. You needed pure skin to allow your body to breathe. This was consistent of a true runner; a fun runner was a different matter. John was no athlete, but he liked to run.

"Now, unless you can pull out one of those fun-run costumes to match the make-up you're wearing, Miss Jones, I suggest you rethink." John left the questions at that for now as it had given him enough for that moment.

"DS Walker, will you arrange for Miss Jones to be taken to the station? Much better environment there," said John in a calm manner walking up to Wren. "We need a full statement, all the detail," said John. "Perhaps it will help Miss Jones to trace her steps," John said loud enough for Sophie to hear. "And maybe re-think the trainer situation!"

"Accompany where...? Where...? When?" said Sophie in a confused state, butting in on what she had just heard. "Am I being arrested? I'm being arrested, aren't I? I had nothing to do with this... it's fucked up, this is... fucked up," Sophie said again.

"No, Miss Jones, you'll be helping us with our enquiries, we need to put the pieces of the puzzle together," John said, "starting with the facts," he said again. "Wren..." said John.

"Okay, sir," Wren said. No more words were needed as Wren understood.

In police work you could have conversations with a colleague without having them; it was a kind of reduced speech that only the person you worked with understood. Anyone outside that circle would not have a clue what you meant. John used this a lot with his team. Kept it quick and short.

John was an excellent detective. He gave out a manner of calm and a sense that he was a guy who could be played and hadn't a clue what he was doing, but don't be fooled – he was a great detective. He had a mind that could track the slightest of detail, like a bloodhound chasing the scent of a fox. John had spotted the clean trainers the moment he looked at Sophie from near the Audi, John had watched her conversations with Wren, and he had looked intently at her, studying her complexion. *The make-up, the clean shoes, the gold chain... not consistent for a runner, especially at 7 am with a partner and kid at home,* John thought.

"DS Walker, escort Miss Jones to her house first so she can check in on her child and see her partner," John said. "I expect they will be wanting to know you're all right, Miss Jones, check and see if there are any other trainers sat near the entrance, Wren," John finished with, knowing this would get Sophie thinking.

Nothing from Sophie but a look of disbelief on her face. She looked as if she had been cheating at cards and had been caught fair and square in the act. She didn't reply to John but sank back down on the seat of the police car. John could see the look on her face change.

"Sir," said Wren, grabbing John's arm and stopping him in his tracks. "She was just out running," Wren said, looking behind John at Sophie now sat back on the seat of the police car hunched over and cuddling the red blanket. Wren looked around John's figure, moving her black hair from her eyes.

"She wasn't running, Wren, nor was she alone," John said in a quiet voice.

"How can you be sure?" Wren said to John, still clinging on to his arm and looking up at him from behind the black hair still hanging in the way of her eyes.

"Call it a feeling," said John raising a smile at Wren but dislodging her hand that had gripped on to his arm like a hawk clutching its prey.

"A feeling, a feeling? You're the best, " said a voice to John.

"Leave it out," John said out loud, laughing.

"Sorry, sir?" said Wren.

"Nothing, Wren, carry on," John said.

A crime scene is like a sponge cake; from the moment you stand looking at the cake, you make a mental picture. The look, the colour, the smell, its construction. Was this person a full-blown cook, experienced in baking, or were they chancing it! The closer you get the more the cake exposes itself. And once you take a bite and break through the layers, the different flavours and tastes become apparent; the tiniest flavour revealing something different. The soft, jammy centre, what jam was used? Why strawberry not blackberry? This was how John looked at crime scenes. From the moment they turned down the street, John was calculating. He was peeling back the layers; he was tasting the environment. He was checking the initial look of the cake, he was feeling the edges with his fingers, looking at the jam and colour... Every part and feel of that first encounter told John a lot. He knew detail before he cut into the cake. He liked to get to a scene as early as possible before the net closed in and evidence faded. People forgot the tiniest of detail and it was John's job to peel that back. On this occasion, as John suspected, there was more to this sponge cake than met the eye.

A sponge cake, triple layered with different flavoured filling. Made numerous ways, no sponge the same. Everyone makes them differently. It's not until you cut the first slice that it reveals the different layers and tells you a bit about the person who made it. If overlooked the outer layers of the sponge will be hard like a shell. Similar to people, cut through the layers before you judge – Jenny Miste, kitchen goddess.

10

It was 10.30 am, the sun was settling in the sky and the once quiet park was bustling with life. There were lines of people at the entrance pushing and shouting, trying to get a glimpse of what behold them. As if by magic the papers were there. John could never understand how the hell they got to a place so quickly. He would joke that they had their own cameras patrolling the city, and in the event that something was spotted, a large BAT signal would flare into the sky; reporters would fly to the scene in caps and masks... it always made John smile. He treated them with the contempt they deserved. Over the years with the Wolf case they had been a pain in the arse. On numerous occasions John had found himself as top headline...

'Bumbling Miste, no nearer to the truth' – *Leicester Mercury*.

'Miste wife mauled by the Wolf' – *Leicetser Port*

Amazing how insensitive they could be to get a story... *Tossers*, John would think.

The flashing cameras of the press lit up the air and John wiped at his brow. The cold of the morning started to settle. The tiny rain droplets clinging to the grass on the large hill gently popped in the sun. A distant dog could be heard barking.

John walked up to the tent and the sergeant passed him some blue gloves and some overshoes. John put the blue gloves on and lifted a leg to fit the overshoes.

"Sergeant, give me a hand, will you?" John said, balancing on one leg with his arm out as if catching a fly.

"Yes, sir," said the sergeant, walking over to John and offering a shoulder for him to balance on while he put on the overshoes.

"Messy, messy... take a breath..." said the voice in John's head.

John pushed through the flaps of the large white tent. He bent as he walked through so he didn't bang his head on the top pole. The flaps shut behind John.

When you first enter a crime scene there can be several things that hit you; the devastation can unfold itself in numerous ways. It can be a smell, a sight, or even the faces of the other officers. No scene is the same. John stood just inside the door to the tent, the flaps shut tight behind him and the busy scene on the car park seemed like a different time or space. The tent was large, much larger than it looked outside. The police had been busy covering the area to ensure not even the slightest of glances could be taken. The tent covered a space of around thirteen feet square, the six floodlights on their yellow frames standing, lighting up the space. They were spread evenly. You would think the distance between them had been measured. The power leads ran around the perimeter and out to a small generator that was chuntering away just outside. The hole the leads passed through was taped shut. The noise of the generator dampened out the busy environment. The light from the floods bounced off the white tent and heated it up like a dance hall. Sections of the grass verge were covered by the tent and the particles of water John saw outside were nowhere to be seen inside. The gravel was dry, dried out from the damn lights that the police insisted on having in such a compact space, John would grumble...

John took his chewing gum out of his mouth and placed it back in the silver foil he had in his left pocket. He folded it neatly and put it in his back pocket. John looked at his watch (10.30 am) and lifted his head. John looked from left to right surveying the scene: the two forensic officers dusting at the floor; the small yellow identification flags placed carefully around the area. The tent was large enough to have a small walk area round the perimeter, an area that let you survey without disrupting the affected surface. There were two officers standing to the left of John; one was a man short and fat with a shirt and tie. His shirt was light brown and tucked into his trousers, unevenly. He wore the blue overshoes, although one was half hanging off and allowing his back heel to mark the ground... His arms were hairy and very brown, as if he spent all summer abroad or under a sunbed. His armpits were wet, his balding head glistening from the floodlights and wet from the heat. He wore a gold chain around his neck with some sort of writing that John couldn't make out. The woman next to him could have been his spit double, if she wasn't a woman, John thought. The only difference was she had hair! The sweat and the clothes very similar. John thought they must have both got dressed in the dark, and even worse... shared the same tailor...

They both stood surveying the scene in front of them.

"DI Miste," John said, looking at them both standing side by side looking down at the ground.

The small fat man turned and looked at John. He held a handkerchief to his nose and mouth to cover the smell from the waste in the bins.

In the police's haste, they had covered two of the car park bins as part of the scene. Although they were further back, they fell within the warmed tent, the overflowing, putrid contents heating in the floodlights' glare. The smell penetrated the air and grabbed at the nostrils. John had a strong stomach. Nothing really fazed him as he had seen too much in his life... even at thirty-nine. The officers in front of him were late forties... John knew he was in a different league the moment he saw them.

"DI Jackson and DS Tims," said the fat man to John, pointing at DS Tims using his head rather than his hands. John struggled to understand DI Jackson but put it down to the handkerchief. He didn't even remove this to give his name!

"Bloody tragedy… bloody mess… Someone's got a hell of a paper trail with this one," said DI Jackson.

John stood silent and didn't answer. He looked at the scene ahead of him, he looked at the placement, the trail, the layout, and he knew almost instantly the Wolf had attacked again.

11

John had seen this type of cop before, he knew it well. The type that does as little as possible to avoid the paperwork. The type that rushes a scene because they want to get home to the TV, or pub if the case may be. John could tell their characters instantly. He had taken in their detail the moment he entered the tent.

The body that lay in front of him was a woman, mid-twenties with long brown hair. Her body was face down with her left leg bent sharply to the left. The bend was so severe it had fractured the bone and pushed it clean out of the skin. The body was naked. Around her neck was a chain, gold with some sort of pendant that John couldn't see. There were no clothes of any kind. The forensic team was busy taking photos and surveying the body. There was no smell and John knew she hadn't been there long. There was black and blue bruising to her torso. Her head was loose on her shoulders, nearly decapitated but spinal tissue hanging on for dear life. John moved closer to the body to get a better look.

Her arms were spread out to the side of her and her hands, like her head, were hanging loose on the tendons. The blood had seeped into the ground. The gravel around her was deep red.

By now, John was kneeling down near the torso, studying it intently. He looked up and down the body, rubbing his stubble whilst deep in thought. He looked at the gravel and surveyed the scene in front of him. The forensic team walked round John busy taking shots, the click and flash from the cameras intense. John wiped the sweat from his brow using the back of his hand.

"What do we know about the victim?" John said to the two detectives who were still standing watching him. They watched him as if he were insane and had polluted their environment.

"What do we know?" John said again, this time looking up at DI Jackson.

"Her name is Carole, Carole… Peters," DI Jackson said with a pause as he quickly looked at his notes in DS Tims' left hand.

"We won't know much more than that until the autopsy is concluded," DI Jackson said again. "She matches the profile of a missing girl from Fleckney, reported a week ago."

John was still kneeling, his left hand on his face and his right hand holding a pen he had taken from Wren's car earlier. His blue gloves were tight on his hands. John was prodding the pen at Carole's fingernails and hands. The DI and DS looked at each other as if to say, 'What is this guy doing?'

"We have been told by our chief that this is your case, and you're to handle it as it links to the Wolf," DS Tims said whilst still covering her mouth with a handkerchief. In fact, one the exact same colour as DI Jackson's.

John let out a 'hmmm' and nodded. "Perhaps it does. Who is to say?" John said to them without looking up. Some shoe prints were present and Forensics had already tagged them ready. This was a messy kill.

"Come on, DS Tims, let's get out of here and leave it to the big shot," said DI Jackson with a frowned expression, the handkerchief so tight at his face that the blood from his hand had run dry.

John didn't move from his position, his eyes still taking in the scene and surveying what was before him. His pen gently lifted the right hand of Carole and exposed the fingernails.

"Oh Carole," John said. "Poor, poor girl…" he said again in a soft, light tone.

The tent flaps opened letting in the glare of the sun and some well needed fresh air. DS Tims and DI Jackson walked out, leaving a shoe cover cleanly in its position. *Fucking arseholes*, John thought as he watched them barge out. At the same time, Wren walked in nearly flooring the DI.

"Whoops… something on fire?" she said as they passed her. Her feet had the blue overshoes on and the gloves sat tidily on her hands.

"That didn't last long then," Wren said as she stood with her back to the tent flaps. "The guys at the station were betting ten minutes' max but I knew better!" she said again.

"What you talking about, Wren?" said John, lifting himself up from the kneeling position and wiping the gravel from the same position on his knees as it was earlier.

"The other two from South Leicester… think I won that bet," said Wren with a smile on her face.

Wren was right; the two officers from South Leicester had lasted five minutes with John. He had this ability to really piss people off, he was known for it. South Leicester hated him. He had worked on their ghost cases a few times in the force's 'force to force' working strategy. To say John wasn't requested for many times would be an understatement. It wasn't what he said but the fact he seemed to get cases cracked, cases that no one else could. *Dog with a bone*, Wren thought. This pissed other cops off.

Ghost cases – The shit that no one else can crack, the ones every now and then the force pulls up and looks at, showing we are doing our bit… yeah, like Mark… ghost case…

"It's all ours now," said Wren to John.

"Okay, I want the autopsy as soon as possible, make sure Jacob gets this moving," said John.

Jacob was the coroner at John's force; a tall, thin guy. He

worked on all John's cases and he knew his stuff. John never told him but he liked him. He worked in the mortuary room at Leicester Hospital, a place John had spent numerous evenings. He had a sense of humour that a guy shouldn't have in his line of work; suppose it kept him sane from the crap he saw.

Wren had spoken to Jacob previously. He had visited the site earlier to survey the scene and arrange the move. The forensic team needed to do their bit before the body could be moved. Wren spotted him while John was at the car.

John walked towards Wren, licking his lips with a deep sense of thought about him.

"What is it?" said Wren. "What's wrong?" she said again.

"Something isn't right," John said.

John walked and stood near Wren who was still standing near the tent flaps trying to keep some clean air rolling round her and the light of the floods off her face.

"Look at the scene, the way she is lying; there isn't one bit of dirt or gravel on her. No sign of struggle. Her nails, clean cut and nothing broken. In full view of the road and cameras," John said again. "Even her chain is in place," John said still looking at the scene in front of him. "And the leg? Well, that's just bizarre. There are foot prints near the body, very very messy... not like the Wolf!" John said

"So?" said Wren. "He was disturbed by Miss Jones, perhaps?"

"Could be," said John. "But how the hell can you get a body to this position, without any marks or sign of struggle in the gravel, or noise to be heard? Just a few prints from a boot or shoe. Look at their position, there is only one pair, in and out," John said. "The CCTV looks straight at the car park," John said. "Big risk... big, big risk... Not only that but I don't think he cut the limbs here. If he did the blood splattering would have been more pronounced. Nothing on the grass, not a sign. Only dry blood that ran from the body after the event," said John.

"What are you saying, that he put the body here like that,

all the parts hanging loose. It's not possible – the body would have been flapping around like a rag doll," said Wren pointing at the torso. "And who is to say he didn't cut her here as the blood is all over the gravel," Wren said.

"When you cut at a body, like when you cut into meat… parts of the skin and tissue come loose and fall to the surface. The veins full of blood burst like a balloon full of water," John said.

"If the Wolf cut the torso here, the evidence would have been greater. It would be like a blood bath. All we have is a small section of the blood that was left in the body, and a few boot prints. said John.

"The position and placing just isn't right," said John, rubbing his head.

"Think back, Wren, to the other scenes; they all had a purpose… Why here? Why now? Leaving prints in the ground, its not like the Wolf at all."

"We can't speculate, sir, until we have the full report," said Wren.

"It's too loose, too loose," said John.

Wren's phone started to vibrate in her pocket. It brought her back into reality and away from the scene in front of her. John stood still, thinking deeply and gently taking off the gloves as he looked at the bins, the gravel and the scene again. He thought about Miss Jones… all swirling around his head, different pieces of a large puzzle. He thought about the prints that the team were slowly dusting.

"DS Walker," Wren said, answering the phone. "Yes ma'am… Yes ma'am… we will, yes." Wren put the phone down and placed it back in her long coat pocket.

All she needs is a grim reaper blade and she would have the perfect look, John thought letting out a small laugh.

"That was the chief. She wants us back at the station to go over the scene."

John chucked his gloves at the ground and left the tent. The sun hit him in the face and the bustling of the crowd caught his attention. He shook his head as if to make them feel like bad children. The voice inside his head was as clear as day: *Don't leave me here like this, please I'm cold... help me, help me.*

John stopped in his tracks, turned and walked back to the tent. Wren stayed exactly where she was bemused by John's actions. She stood in the middle of the car park with her Audi to her side.

He marched to the tent with the gravel crunching under his feet. As he got to the tent flaps he slowed down and opened it gently, just enough for him to squeeze his head in and look at the scene. Forensics were still busy, their white suits and masks reflecting the floodlights. To the right stood a woman, naked and shaking, her arms crossed in front of her breast and her feet bare. The gold chain on her neck glittered against the floodlights, the words 'Best Friend' as clear as day on the pendant. Her green eyes were prominent on her face. The matted hair and tears strewn on her face showed her suffering.

"It's okay," said John, "it's okay... I won't leave you... It's fine..." The tears in his eyes welled up... "I'll sort this... I will... you can trust me," John said, his head still sticking through the tent door. At that point one of the forensic team looked up at him.

"Did you say something, sir?" he said.

John paused...

"Ah, yes... The chain, there are words on it... best friend, I think!" said John stuttering.

The team stopped what they were doing and looked over at Carole, the chain was buried under her head and couldn't be seen from its position. They leaned in to get a better look but still couldn't see any wording. DC1, as the team member was called, looked back at John with a puzzled face. No words were needed.

At that point Wren prodded him in the back and broke his attention. John jumped.

"Fuck sake, Wren, don't creep up on me like that," John said, tears still wet in his eyes.

"Who were you speaking to, forensics?" said Wren.

"That's right," John said looking at her. "That's right."

John turned back and looked in the tent. The young woman John saw so clearly had gone. The strewn body was still in place, the forensic team as busy as before. DC1 was still looking at John with a puzzled expression; you could see his mind wurling at what the DI had just said, and at how he could have seen any words on a chain that was covered. The body was lifted several hours later, the gold chain that sat on her neck was taken and bagged for evidence by the team. They could only get to this once Carole's body was moved.

On examination, the chain was found to have the words 'Best friend' on it, just as John had said.

12

Leicester's serious crime unit was on the third floor of the imposing police headquarters. The Leicestershire force was established in a village called Enderby, just near the motorway. Good for access all over the city. It had large gates and a large fence that went all round the perimeter. The large blue sign sat high on chrome feet. In summer, it cast a shadow over the front grass, almost blackening all the ground-floor offices at the front. You had to have the lights on full all day. The fluorescent tubes buzzed in the heat. The building was constructed in the fifties, although it had been extended over the years to incorporate all the different divisions. The Leicester force was the headquarters for all the branches including the south. The other branches around the city reported to HQ on several occasions throughout the month; the suited and booted marching in with their briefcases scrutinising every penny spent on a monthly basis. John was glad he didn't have to deal with this bullshit.

Wren and John pulled up at the gate, Wren withdrew her ID and pressed the window button. The car window started to lower with a clunk but stopped halfway. Wren frantically tapped at the window button.

"What the bloody hell is wrong with this now?" she said as she continued pressing the window button.

John was deep in thought from the scene, his mind going

over every detail. He was that focused he hadn't even spotted they were at HQ, or that Wren was pushing frantically at the window button. Wren pushed the intercom and heard it buzz into life.

"Leicestershire HQ, can I help you?" said the voice on the other end.

"It's DS Walker and DI Miste. Can you let me through, please?" Wren said, stretching her neck to ensure the sound penetrated through the gap in the window.

"Wren, when will you get that damn car fixed?" said the voice on the intercom.

"Just let me through, please," Wren said again.

There was a clunk and the large black electric gates opened. They were slow and opened as if you had just woken them from a long sleep.

Wren drove the Audi to the car park at the back. It was full of police-marked vehicles but she managed to find a space. She pulled the car to a stop, pulled on the handbrake, and switched off the engine.

"Sir, we are here," Wren said.

"What? Ah yes… perfect," John said in a daze.

They both stepped from the car and headed to the large metal door up a small disabled ramp. Just before Wren put the code in she turned and said to John,

"So, when you going to come out with me for some dinner?"

"What?" John said.

"Dinner, you know… food…" said Wren in a sarcastic tone.

"I know what you meant," said John as they both stood near the large, metal door. The sun glared of it straight into John's eyes.

"I'm too old for you, Wren," John said. "I'm flattered, but our relationship just won't work," John said looking at her and raising a smile.

"I didn't mean like that, sir," Wren said in an embarrassed

70

manner. "Just, you know, you don't get out much now... Claire... you know... is... well... passed," she said hesitating along the way.

"I'm kidding, Wren. A drink sounds good, and maybe I'll push to a sandwich!" John said.

Just at that point the door came alive and unlocked. John and Wren walked in.

13

The office is an affair with a gorgeous young woman: it keeps you out all hours; it takes all your attention; it drains you; it takes every one of your thoughts. When it's done, it spits you back out... nothing left... – Claire Miste.

John and Wren got out of the lift on the third floor. The corridor in front of them was long, with doors leading off at every turn and people dashing about here, there and everywhere. At the end, in the distance, there was a cheese plant and a water dispenser, just before the sharp left to John's office. The cheese plant had been there for as long as John could remember and every now and then he added some water. You could tell who had fed it each day as the colour of the leaves changed. Monday – Martin, as his coffee was strong; Tuesday – Jack, as his tea was weak. That plant had some variety... damn thing kept growing and growing. It always put a smile on John's face. The ceiling in the corridor had runs of tiles with bright LED fittings in them. They were so bright you couldn't stare at them long. They made the walls and floors look shit. They had been upgraded as part of the 'saving money' initiative which had caused hell in John's office as they had to cover the crime detail for risk of exposure. Pain in the arse!

"Miste," a voice said behind John and Wren as they walked up the corridor towards the plant.

"Ma'am," John said as he turned and stopped. "You go ahead

and get the team ready," John said to Wren, indicating to her with his head to carry on going.

The DCI was Mary Claridge – she was tall and very pretty. She had that aura about her that John did; she always wore high heels and her hair was down to her shoulders, thick and dark. She was early forties but looked early thirties. Big chest, and she knew it! Her husband had dumped her the year before and shacked up with the neighbour.

According to the rumours, Mary came home one evening and found them in her bed stark naked and at it like rabbits.

Following that it was said that he spent some time inside for fraud, some tax issues, although it was thought that Mary had something to do with this. They hadn't spoken since and he lived in a one-bed flat in St Martins. Poor bastard… wouldn't wish that on anyone.

"So, Miste, what do we know?" said DCI Claridge.

"It's messy, ma'am, very messy… looks like the Wolf…but…"

"But what…?" she said.

"I'm not sure yet, need to get the detail down."

DCI Claridge was leaning in hoping to pry more from John but he kept it to his chest.

"Need a full report on my desk the moment you have it. My arse is being chewed with this. Sixteen murders and no suspect… bleeding hell, John, give me something."

"Look, ma'am, just tell them there is a connection and we are working on it… as soon as I've had a chance to go over the detail, I'll let you know." John turned and headed towards the plant. He closed his eyes and took a deep breath. It pissed him off being rushed; he needed time to check every detail. He needed time to contemplate his moves.

"You'd better, John, as it's your arse on the line as well," the chief yelled, her voice rattling off the walls.

John stopped at the vending machine just before the end of the corridor. It was old and had seen better days. He picked at

73

his left pocket and found some loose change, totalling a couple of pounds. John stood counting and gently let them slip from his fingers to the vending machine slot. It ate them like a hungry dog.

John pressed for a cheese sandwich. It was 12.30 pm and his stomach was in knots, the night before was well behind him now but his stomach still suffering.

The machine started to turn and the sandwich moved forward but just at the edge it stopped.

"Not a-bleeding-gain? Every bloody time I—"

"You okay, sir?" Wren said.

"This bloody machine, I'm sure it's got it in for me, does this every time…"

Wren walked up to the machine and gave it a sharp kick. John's sandwich dropped into the slot below with a thud, along with a chocolate bar he didn't ask for.

"Serves you right," John said to the machine, grabbing at the contents it released.

14

The serious crime office was a small space but intimate. It had a high ceiling fully tiled, the LED panels glowing white, and a carpet that had been there since time began. Tattered and worn.

It had a smell that you couldn't explain, a smell that was familiar but yet not unpleasant. There were rows of desks with computers and phones. One wall was covered in windows and was south facing; it got the sun most days and today was no exception. The blinds were pulled half down to keep the glare off the monitors. The large fan radiators blew and banged under there skirting covers. If the walls could talk… John walked in and went straight to the small room in the corner. It had a window looking out into the office and a small door. There was one desk, two chairs and a filing cabinet. The paperwork on John's desk was high and almost covered his view. He could just about get to his computer, his phone, stapler, tape and pens lost under the files. There were certificates on the walls in frames and some photos of John shaking hands with numerous people in the force from one time or another. A picture of John and Claire sat on his desk with a blue sky and sea in the background.

John sat at his desk and slumped into his leather seat, the leather bending and folding under his weight. He put the cheese sandwich and chocolate bar on the desk and opened his shirt a few buttons. He puffed his cheeks as if back at home in his safe zone. John opened the drawer to his desk and picked up a pill pot, he looked over the paperwork, stretching his neck, then looked down at the bottle. He opened the lid... Empty... Shit!

This was John's spare emergency stash. He hadn't taken his pills now for days and the voices and images were returning fast.

"Bugger it," John said to himself. He put the bottle back in the drawer and closed, and opened, and closed it several times until he counted twelve. That settled John and he knew it was closed correctly.

John picked up the cheese sandwich, opened the wrapper and went to take a bite.

"Sir, we are ready when you are..." Wren said peeking round the door.

John just managed to get the sandwich to his lips, he just managed to lift it high enough to smell the onion...

John walked into the office and stood in front of the whiteboard. There were numerous names and links, maps and dates. Claire's name was on there as the Wolf's last kill with a copy of the note by her picture. Wren had already started placing names and links for Carole on the board.

"Okay guys, okay... what do we know so far?" said John munching at his sandwich and the crumbs dropping to the floor...

"Well?" said John as no one spoke; they were too busy watching John eat.

"Right, yes, well. We have a woman, Carole Peters, the deceased, murdered somewhere between 2 am and 5 am... still waiting for the full detail from Jacob," Wren said.

"Okay, what else?" said John standing eating his sandwich.

"We have a witness of sorts, Miss Jones; called in the body, running we think, but we need to confirm."

"Okay, Wren," said John. "Clive, have you checked the CCTV yet? Anything to report?" said John.

"I'm on it. It's being pulled and sent over to me now; should have it shortly," Clive said. Clive was part of John's detective team; in his late fifties; always wore a tattered old suit. Decent guy and good at his job.

"Don't just sit there, Clive, push them!" John said loudly. He said it so loudly he choked on a piece of his sandwich.

"Can someone get me a tea please? Something to wash this waste down with…" John said again coughing.

John threw the sandwich into the bin to the side of him. He had almost finished it but the smallest section remained. It hit the bin hard, making it rock from side to side.

"Here you go, sir," said Chloe, holding a cup of tea in front of him.

"Thank you," said John, taking a deep sip of the contents.

Cup still in hand, John continued…

"Right, we have a body of a young female, consistent with the Wolf's taste. She fits his type and age range. The difference is this time something went wrong," John said turning so his back was to the team and he was standing looking at the whiteboard. He was so tall that the team moved to one side so they could still see the board. They all sat on a sofa in the middle of the office. It was a thinking zone and a place where they discussed items. It was an old blue thing that could sit eight to ten people easily. Wren sat in the middle of Clive and Chloe listening to John speak.

"The Wolf always kills his victim, leaves different body parts. No evidence… no witness, nothing," John says pointing at the names and pictures of the victims on his board. "What happened this time to make it different?" John said again with a leading question.

"He was disturbed," Wren said chewing at her pen. "Miss Jones, it must have been her," Wren said again.

"I agree, Wren, but we have inconsistencies. She called it in at 7.30 am and was out running at 7 am according to her. So why would the Wolf drop the body as he did around 2-5 am and not finish his work. Who disturbed him at that time?" John said. "Or... did she see him, he fled... leaving prints, meaning we have a key witness?" John said.

"Yes, but the early info from Jacob indicates the body was there around 2-5 am," said Clive.

"No Clive, it indicates the death was between 2-5 am on that day, it indicates we have the start of the Wolf's process... the start of his plan, and something went wrong," John said. Clive nodded in agreement.

"I don't believe we should have found the body there at all, I believe she was dumped there in haste. Unfinished work... unfinished job... come on, Wolf... what are we missing? This is our shot, guys. After all the victims, this is our shot to nail the bastard!" John said still sipping at his hot tea and looking at the whiteboard.

"Sir, sorry to disturb you but we have a Miss Jones in custody. Shall I take her to interview room 1?" the officer said, standing at the door to the crime unit, looking scared to cross the threshold.

"Yes, take her through, Sergeant," John said. "Clive, hit the CCTV, check every detail. Everything," said John. "Chloe, I want you to go back to the scene, speak to forensics; somehow, some way, he got that body to the car park. It didn't fly in! Go, go, guys, let's get moving!" John said getting his team from off the sofa.

The office became busy, the detectives all moving to their positions. Wren left the room with the sergeant to go and set up interview room 1. Clive positioned himself at his desk and began to tap at the computer. Chloe left, taking her coat, bag and keys. She was heading to Watermead.

"Chloe, can you do me a favour?" John said still holding his cup and his back to the office.

"Yes, sir, of course," said Chloe.

John turned and walked closer to Chloe.

"Can you trace the steps of Miss Jones and let me know the time it takes to get from number six to the scene. Walk it Chloe, and call DS Walker with what you find. I want her shoes for evidence and we need to rule out anything at her house that matches the prints. Her Partner as well. Would you do that please?" said John.

"Of course, sir," said Chloe.

She was in awe of John; he was an imposing force and the way he unravelled cases was incredible.

"And someone get me something on our victim, she hasn't just appeared out of thin air!" John said, shouting into the room.

15

Interview room 1 was being set up. It was one of the small rooms along the corridor. It had just enough room for a small table, recorder, and a camera placed in the top corner. You only knew this was on by the red light glowing against its lens. The LED panels glowed brightly on the brown tabletop. John knocked on the door and walked in. Wren was already sitting facing Miss Jones. Wren had a small file open with notes in that she had made through the day. Her mobile was on the table. John slid the occupied sign on the door and closed it behind him.

He pulled out the chair beside Wren and sat himself down. He fiddled with the chair until it was in place. The white teacup sat on the table in front of John. John hadn't looked at Miss Jones yet as he was too busy settling himself. Wren was looking at him patiently. She had now taken off her coat and looked more petite than ever. Her shirt was tucked in her trousers and one button open at the top exposing her white skin below. Her hair was still flat to her head and in immaculate position. John rubbed his hands through his long brown hair and smiled at Miss Jones, who by this time was just staring at John with a blank expression. She wore a small pink coat that covered her tight running clothes. Her shoes had been taken and placed in an evidence bag, and she was wearing Police issue white shoes. Too big for her feet.

"Okay, Miss Jones, comfy?" John said, smiling at her.

"Yes, fine, thank you, fine!" she said with a blank manner.

"Would you like something to drink before we start?" John said pointing at his cup which sat steaming on the table.

Miss Jones looked at the cup then back at John. It took her a moment then she said:

"Why am I here? I told you lot everything at the park... This is bullshit... total bullshit..." she said, crossing her arms in front of herself and settling back into the seat with a thump.

"Just routine, Miss Jones, need to fill some blanks," Wren said.

"Would you like a solicitor, Miss Jones?" John said looking straight at her and tapping at the file Wren had slipped under his hand.

"Why would I need a solicitor? Am I under arrest?"

"Not at all," said John. "Not at all. You're just helping us with our enquires," John said still tapping the paperwork.

"Okay, Wren," John said indicating at the recorder on the table, "let's begin."

"DI Miste and DS Walker, time is 2 pm on Monday, 21st April, interview with Miss Jones."

John, without a shadow of doubt, was one of the best interviewers on the force. He could make a person feel calm and relaxed, then somehow prize the most important information from them that even they didn't know they knew. He had a gift... incredible to watch.

John sat for a moment, the tape running, looking at the notes in front of him. He read the information gently. He put his hand in his pocket and pulled out the silver wrapper he had put there earlier. He opened it, took out the gum and put it back in his mouth chewing slowly, one hand to his head, resting it on his hand, and the other turning the pages. This wasn't a very nice habit as the gum would have been hard and tasteless, it made Wren feel sick everytime he did it.

"WELL… why am I here?" said Miss Jones getting more frustrated by the minute.

"Sorry, Miss Jones, yes, I'll get to the point for you. You told the officers you were out running, you told them you spotted the body at 7.30 and called it in. Is that correct, Miss Jones?"

"Yes, that's correct…I've told you this already!"

"Do you run often?" said John.

"Most days. Why?"

"And your child, Poppy, do you leave her alone in the house or is she with someone?" John said while still reading his notes.

"She is with my partner; he isn't her father but he is a good man. I've been with him years. What is this all about?" said Miss Jones, this time leaning forward on the table. "I need to get back; I need to get home," said Miss Jones.

"Okay, Sophie, let me get to the point," John used her first name, "I don't believe you were running, nor do I believe you are a runner. You don't dress like a runner and your make-up and clean shoes are a giveaway.

"I want to know why the hell a girl of your age, with a kid and fella at home, would want to be out at that time in the morning in running gear, when you're not planning to run!"

"It was 7 am, you make it sound like it was midnight," said Sophie.

"You misunderstand me, Sophie. You found the body earlier, didn't you, as you were out earlier than you're letting on? You rang it in later to cover your arse!" John said, looking her straight in the face. Wren was listening contently and also staring at Sophie.

There was a long silence, John chewed his gum and sat back in his seat with his arms crossed. Wren sat with her arms on the table. Sophie sat with her head in her hands.

"I want the truth; no lies, the truth," said John. There was a silence that seemed to last for a while.

"I found her at 3.45 am," Sophie said, not even looking up from her hands. "I'm having a fling with a guy down the road, we meet on the park a few nights per week... it's... you know... it's sex and it's good... he makes me feel alive inside!" she said, looking at Wren. John looked at her and nodded. "You won't tell my partner will you?" asked Sophie

"And?" said John.

"We were the other side of the bank near the grass, you know... together..."

"What, on the grass?" John said.

"No, there is a bench, we sit there and you know, well... I'm sure I don't have to spell it out!" said Sophie, raising her hands.

"We heard a noise, and it was a woman screaming; not loud screams but kind of muffled, you know like if you scream under a duvet!" Sophie said looking at John.

"And what did you do?" Wren asked.

"Well, I pushed Martin off, and pulled up—"

"Spare us the full detail, Sophie, please... just the facts!" John butted in, getting annoyed with the time it was taking her.

"We heard a noise so we both got off the bench, walked up the stone steps and looked over the bank," said Sophie.

"What was the time exactly?" said John.

"3.30-3.40 am ish," said Sophie.

John was still tapping his pen against the notes in front of him and taking in every detail Sophie was saying.

"We had nothing to do with this, nothing... just wrong place and the wrong time," Sophie said, raising her voice.

"What did you see?" John said again.

"It was dark as the street lights don't go that far. We take a small torch... you know... so you can see your way and all that... anyway, we climbed to the top and I had my torch and I switched it on."

"Just backing up a moment," said John. "How did you know the time? You don't have a watch on."

"Martin wears a watch, he looked at his watch and told me," said Sophie.

"Okay... continue," said John.

"I switched the torch on and there was a van, like a camper van parked next to the two bins, just outside the car park... you know, where your tent thing was... it had blacked-out windows but you could see the light round the edges. The noise was coming from that."

"Did you see the plates?" Wren said.

"No, it was dark," said Sophie.

"We were about to go back to the bench when the side door opened and a woman fell out."

"What do you mean... fell out?" said John, listening carefully.

"You know... tumbled out... not like pushed, but fell out... at a funny angle..."

"Was she screaming? Was she dressed?" John asked.

"Her mouth was open; it's hard to say... she kind of looked drunk... not in distress... more drunk," said Sophie. "Her leg sort of bent behind her as she fell but she didn't scream so I thought nothing of it," she said again.

"Did you see anyone pull her back in?" John said leaning forward as if waiting for his prize horse to cross the line.

"No, sorry... we just turned quick, switched off the torch, and went back to the bench," said Sophie. "It was none of our business, you know... why should we...? Well, you know!"

There was a silence in the room. John and Wren sat quietly looking at each other and Sophie sat with her arms folded again.

"Look, we were not to know that she would be killed, were we? We don't have much time together and have to grab every minute, me and Martin... bleeding hell, it's not our fault, you know. We didn't see anyone else so assumed she was drunk!"

Another silence followed and John looked at her, bewildered.

"Interview terminated at 2.35pm," John said, pushing the stop button on the recorder.

"Is that it? Can I go now? Jesus... you won't tell Phil, will you? It's complicated," said Sophie, looking at John and Wren.

"That's your job, Sophie," said John. "We will need to verify your details with Martin. So, we will need to speak to him," John said, closing his note file. "Next time, I would think twice on where you shack up; that could have been you!" John said.

Sophie looked blank, John's words dancing in her mind. He had hit a nerve.

"Wren, escort Miss Jones to reception," John said.

"Oh yes, one more thing, Miss Jones," John said as Sophie and Wren were about to leave, "when you saw her fall from the van, did she have a necklace on? Now, think carefully please."

Sophie paused and said, "Yes... yes, she did. It was gold."

"And when you left the bench, did Martin see the body also?" John said.

"No, he goes one way and I go the other. I climbed up the bank looked over and there she was, it was on my way back and I was alone. That's why I switched the torch off and headed back down. I didn't want to get involved!" said Sophie

"You didn't scream?" said John. "So, you just left her there, in the cold and dark... went home back to your partner, then called it in at 7.30?" John said in an irritated manner.

"Look, I know how it sounds; shit, I feel terrible. I know it's wrong... it shook me up. I didn't go to bed. I sat in the kitchen in tears... never get that sight from my mind... never," said Sophie, shaking her head. "I was too shocked to scream, I just went home."

"Did you run?" John asked.

"No, I didn't run," said Sophie.

"Escort her out, Wren," John said indicating at the door with his file. "And check the bank for footprints to verify her story. Check with forensics and see if they found any tyre tracks that match what Sophie has told us as well," John finished.

"Will do, sir," said Wren as she escorted Sophie out the room

16

It was a cold morning, the spring sun from the day before
had faded and the clouds covered the sky. The early morning
sounds of the streets could be heard banging and bumping in
the background. The lights from the city lit the sky. It was 6
am and John was already in a cab on his way to the infirmary.
He wore a new clean shirt and had his coat firmly zipped to
his neck. He had planned to meet Jacob the day before but
time was against him. John had spent a few more hours in his
office after the interview, contemplating the detail. He liked to
be alone to think. His small notebook was full. Page after page
used in one day. It must have been way past 7 pm when he
left, the voices in his head and the images all adding to John's
thoughts. The images had got worse last night and John had
trouble sleeping. He couldn't take the pills at night; they were
too powerful. If he did he just couldn't wake up. A bomb could
go off and John wouldn't know. He had taken them in the past
and Claire had to physically tip him from the bed!

His house was busy…

Claire met him as he walked through the door and so did
Carole. They both talked and chatted in John's kitchen as he
sat in the armchair in the front room. John had sat looking
out of the front blinds at the moon, a glass of beer beside him
and his shirt fully buttoned down. It had been a hard day.
John had seen some shit and almost certainly listened to a

lot of bullshit. The chit-chat, chit-chat from the kitchen was like whispers of noise, jumping round John's head. John lifted the cool glass of beer to his head and closed his eyes... taking deep, long breaths. Last thing John remembered from the evening was Carole telling him she was friends with Claire, both of them hugging and smiling. John couldn't remember the rest. He woke, dressed, in the same armchair, the empty glass beside him, the room silent. The wispers in the dark somehow soothing John to sleep.

Today he was awake, he had taken his pills and even remembered to grab his phone. No voices in his head... peace. There were a few voice messages from the day before glowing on his iPhone; the chief, moaning and groaning... and a few other calls from colleagues.

One call was from John's doctor reminding him it was his check-up that week. John listened to them all as he sat in the cab. John looked out at the city lights as they rumbled by, the delete button being pressed frantically and the phone lighting up John's face. *Fuck them all*, John thought.

The cab came to a stop outside Leicester Infirmary, the place already hustling and bustling.

"What's the damage?" John said to the cab driver as the back of the cab lit up from the small light over John's head.

"£10.45 please, sir," said the cab driver.

John fumbled in his pockets, moving the gum... wallet... phone...

"Here, keep the change," John said, giving the cab driver a £20 note.

John shut the cab door, straightened himself up and headed into the hospital. John knew where to go; he had been here many times before. John didn't like hospitals. He avoided them like the plague... he used to come in through a door at the back but the area was closed for construction... *more ways to piss up government money*, John would think. This meant John had to walk through the hospital and pass all the patients lying on the beds. There were streams of them on trolley beds lining the walls both sides forming a narrow tunnel down the middle. The doctors and nurses flew up and down the middle. You had to walk down this tunnel but snake from side to side; it was like a football game but without the ball, the players barging and tackling their way through. No blinking or speaking, they were in a trance. The thing that always got John was the fact that they never seemed to stop at one of these trolleys; they didn't exist... invisible... *Amazing*, John thought. Jenny was the same during her time in hospital. John remembers his dad kicking off – in fact, he kicked off and complained so badly, they eventually got a room. *Go figure*, John thought.

Hospitals are huge places and the infirmary was no different, it had taken John years to negotiate through the maze of doors and tunnels, years to find the mortuary. You always knew you were heading in the right direction by the faces of the people who passed you by. No expression blank... it was like a completely different place down there.

The road to hell... although we all fucking end up as worm bait, John would think! And the quiet was deafening in itself, just the rattle from the central heating radiators and those damn lights flickering away. The signs only jumped out as you approached the door. It was as if the hospital had hidden them so the trolleys of corpses couldn't see where they were going. There seemed to always be religious signs placed strategically on the walls. *How can that be comfort at this stage... you're dead!* John thought.

John walked through the mortuary door and up to the small reception post. A large lady with brown hair, glasses and bright red lipstick sat behind the desk. Her frame seeped from the sides of the chair due to the weight on her hips. Her fingers tapped at the keyboard in front of her and her eyes fixated on the screen.

"DI Miste… I'm here to see Jacob," John said, holding out his ID card.

The lady from behind the desk stopped tapping, her hands hovering over the keyboard, but her eyes looked up at John. She looked at John then looked past him at the time on the large clock on the bright blue walls. John turned to see what had her attention. A voice then came from deep within her throat like a frog readying itself to let out its song:

"Do you have an appointment? We don't allow visitors before 7.30 am," says the lady.

"Betty, it's John, John Miste… I'm here to see Jacob… it's important."

John looked at Betty and hoped his bright smile and movie complexion would do the trick.

Betty looked at him with her eyes squinted, darting at his face, looking at him as if trying to look at a mug shot and pick her prey. He could feel the poison arrows hitting his skin.

"I just need you to sign for me, please," she said, tapping at a sign-in sheet on her desk.

John looked at Betty, and down at the sheet. John leant down, over the desk and grabbed at the sign-in sheet. John had to lean right over the desk to get this, nearly knocking over the electric pencil sharpener, and his hands met the other side of the desk near the keyboard. Betty wouldn't move, she never did. She made you work… John was sure she liked the way she made people do as she wanted. *If they want it they can bloody work for it,* he would think she thought. She could have pushed the sign-in sheet forward but she never did. *Lazy arse,* John would always think. He was sure if she lifted herself up at least a few times per day, it would help her weight. It didn't matter how many times she saw John, she asked the same bleeding questions. *One day,* John thought, *I'm going to hide in the cleaner's cupboard and watch her come in to work.* He was sure she just sat there day after day twenty-four hours

89

and never moved. He was sure she had no home. How the hell she made the four flights of stairs to get here John never knew... it made him sweat and he was pretty fit. Perhaps she used a trolley and came down in the trolley lift? That thought made him smile.

John signed the sheet.

Betty pressed the buzzer and the door to the right opened, the sign 'Mortuary' clear as day above the glass openings. John pushed the door and walked in. As you walked in, it opened into a large space, stainless steel everywhere. LED lighting glowed off the surfaces and sinks were placed either side.

And those cold, dull floor tiles, what an end... The floor was shiny from the wet mops used to clean the space. If you walked in too fast you could slip right on your arse. On table four was Carole Peters. John pressed the sanitiser on the wall as he entered. He pressed it several times covering his hands in gel. He grabbed the blue pair of gloves from his coat pocket and put them on. They were tight for his hands but he pushed them in. He placed a new piece of gum into his mouth, and walked over to the table.

"John, old boy... can't beat a dead body at this time in the morning, can you?" a voice said from the small office in the corner. It was Jacob.

"Jacob, good to see you here bright and early and full of the joys of spring," John said, looking down at Carole in front of him with his arms crossed.

"Well, you never fail to amaze me, John; the things you bring me... talk about not giving a person much..." said Jacob standing the other side of Carole with a file in his hands.

"Can I have some of that gum?" Jacob said to John.

"Sure," said John grabbing his last one from his pocket and chucking it at Jacob.

Carole's body lay covered with a white sheet, her head had been placed back nearer her shoulders, the once loose tendons removed so her head sat clear of the body. Her hands were on a tray beside her. The identification tags hung on her large toes.

John surveyed the scene.

"So, give me something, Jacob... something," said John.

"Such a waste," said Jacob looking down at Carole lying at peace. "Such a waste."

"Jacob, the facts," said John pulling Jacob back to reality and from his gaze.

Jacob had a funny way about him, a way that if you weren't used to him you could take the wrong way. He was in his late forties and had been married twice; they didn't stick with him long, and he had no kids. His ears were pierced and the tattoos sat clear as day on his arms. He was a rebel and not the character you would expect doing this work. He didn't fit the bill; mind you, John would think, so didn't half the tossers he locked up. Jacob was good at his job.

"Okay, okay, isn't a man allowed a moment now and then...?" Jacob said in a daze.

"Jacob," John said again, pointing at his wristwatch as if waiting for a train.

Jacob opened his file and began to read, John listened.

"Carole Peters, mid-twenties, healthy, confirmed name and DNA, dental records to match. Stomach contents show she hadn't eaten for a day... empty, but she was hydrated. Well-to-do as well, I would say, well-to-do..." Jacob stopped and pulled down the white sheet, revealing the stitching to her chest from the post-mortem.

"Why do you say well-to-do?" John said to Jacob, his hands crossed over his chest.

"If you look at her skin complexion, her nails, well kept... I would even say Botox at some stage on her face. She has had breast implants as well... thousands spent... thousands," Jacob said pointing at the breast. "Very nicely done, I might add," Jacob said, smiling.

John hated this part more than anything; he had a stomach that was hard from the shit he had seen but this part and the environment seemed to always haunt him.

"Jacob, I need facts, tell me something I don't know," John said.

"The cut to her neck and arms were amateur, very amateur. Cut using a sharp blade, same as the other victims, but rushed," Jacob said pointing at the head and hands.

"Can you see these marks at the bottom of the skull? They are made when the blade bites and comes to a complete hold. It was as if he was stopped in his tracks, stopped at the moment before he cut clean through," Jacob finished.

"What do you mean? He stopped himself or he was stopped?" John said, looking at Jacob.

"Stopped by others, I would say. The cuts are consistent with a full stop, not a blade winding down to a complete full stop," Jacob said.

"And the bruising to her back?" John said.

"Old; at least seven days. No fractures but she took a good beating."

"Like an attack beating?" John said.

"No, it was variable bruising, several hits over a space of time to the areas," Jacob said.

"Are we taking training, or sparring?"John said.

"Yes, that would match the bruising and clotting," Jacob said. "Her muscle tone indicates she kept fit."

"The chain round her neck, what do we know on that?" John said, still gazing at the victim in front of him. Jacob walked off to his office. As he did, John bent and pulled the white gown back over Carole's body. A shiver came over him.

"Here we are," Jacob said returning with a clear bag containing a chain.

"Thanks," said John placing the bag into his pocket.

"Excuse me, you'll have to sign for that!" Jacob said, pointing to the bag John had slipped into his pocket. John just smiled and flicked at his hair.

"You were right as well, John," said Jacob

"What do you mean I was right?" said John

"It did say 'Best Friends' on the chain," said Jacob, pointing at John's pocket with his note board.

"Ah yes, lucky guess is suppose!" said John trying to avoid conversation on the chain.

John then continued...

"Were there signs of any sexual contact?" John said.

"No, our girl hadn't been active for a while, had you, dear?" Jacob said patting Carole's head forgetting about the chain conversation.

"The fracture on the leg?" John said pointing down at Carole's leg, breaking Jacob's gaze.

"Nasty, earlier than the head and hand trauma," Jacob said.

"Earlier? How much earlier?" John said, chewing his gum.

"Few hours, I would say; more from a fall," said Jacob.

John took a moment to think, his mind darting over the detail, the van, the witness, prints. Sophie's claims of seeing Carole fall from the van, and bend her leg. It tied in, pieces of the puzzle slipping gently together.

"Ah yes... forgot to mention... the hair," Jacob said.

"What hair?" John said.

"Our Carole was clever, a very clever girl... seems she pulled at our attacker's hair," Jacob said.

John could feel his heart beating in his chest. He closed his eyes for a moment and took in what Jacob had said.

"Are you sure it's not her own hair, or perhaps something she picked up during the process?" John asked, trying to keep his calm.

"Positive. It was positioned in such a way under her nails, that it matches a direct pull. If I was a betting man, I would say she grabbed out and tried to make a run for it," Jacob said. "Mind you..." Jacob said again.

At that point the phone rang in Jacob's office.

"One second, John, one second," said Jacob.

John looked bemused, his arms in the air then slamming against his hips in disbelief. He took some steps back leaning against the stainless-steel sink at the back of him and he chewed his gum with his hands against his face.

What the fuck does all this mean? What the fuck are you trying to tell me? he said in his mind. *Two mistakes... the Wolf doesn't make mistakes... two mistakes?*

By this, John meant Claire; the way she had been placed and the note, the note direct to John indicating desperation. Now Carole... mistakes... differences to the other victims.

The first batch of victims were murdered so perfectly that the evidence just didn't exist. This guy knew his stuff, and in a way John envied him. His ability to cover his tracks. This was and had been the most difficult case John had ever worked on. Not being able to tell the families anything hurt John.

The press were on John's arse week after week, doing their normal to heighten the anxiety of the public by their stupid comments, hanging John out to dry as if he just sat at his desk day in and day out. They never rested, even with Claire, some Internet bastards even writing that John got what he deserved... *Well, they did – we traced them and charged them... fuckers...*

John's mobile rang loudly in his pocket, the vibration jumping John from his thoughts.

"Wren," John said as he answered.

"Sir, up early, weren't you this morning?" Wren said.

"Couldn't sleep. My mind was busy," John said still with his hand against his face.

"You at the hospital?" Wren said.

"Yes, Jacob is filling me in on his void love life," John said looking into Jacob office, smiling with Wren laughing on the line.

Jacob heard this and gave a V-sign to John through the window. John smiled.

"I've got Chloe tracing the park for any signs of car tracks, and she has traced the steps of Sophie. She has checked her trainers as well" said Wren.

"Good," said John. "Have you spoken to Sophie's lover?" John said.

"Yes, he confirms Sophie's story so they are in the clear."

"Okay," said John. "Has the CCTV come back?"

"Yes, and you won't like it," said Wren.

"Go on, hit me with it," John said chewing hard at the gum.

"The cameras lost power the night before; they were down to be fixed two days later. I traced the worksheet to Leicester Council maintenance. It's in a pile higher than your desk, sir," said Wren.

"Doesn't surprise me at all," John said raising a smile and shaking his head.

"What doesn't?" said Wren.

"That he picked this spot, planned the killing to his normal impeccable standards, but it went wrong," said John. "Check all CCTV in the area. We are looking for a camper van with blacked-out windows. Have Clive go over them all with a fine-toothed comb," John said.

"Yes, sir, I'll get on to it," said Wren.

"I'll meet you back at the office. Jacob will email over Carole's details from his file. We need to contact next of kin and arrange formal identification," John said.

"Tread carefully, Wren, this is messy... make sure you contact family liaison"

"Understood," said Wren.

John put the phone down and at the same time so did Jacob.

"Jacob, the 'mind you...' part... can you finish it? The holding on is killing me," John said.

Jacob walked out from his office with another small bag containing the smallest of hair traces. John had to squint to see them clearly.

"I'm running DNA on this now and will get this over once it lands."

John went to grab the bag but Jacob pulled it back.

"This one stays with me, John, I'll let you off with the chain but not this," said Jacob smiling at John.

"Jacob, the hair... come on, man... for fuck sake finish your sentence!" said John.

"Temper, temper," Jacob said, placing the bag of hair on the side counter.

"I was going to say, as my phone rang, mind you she couldn't have grabbed it at a better place."

"Meaning?" John said.

"She grabbed the root so we have blood as well," Jacob announced. "She knew where to grab and how hard."

John pondered and thought, *Yes, this ties up: the bruising, the figure... we have a woman who can defend herself here... interesting the Wolf picked her.*

What John meant by this was it wasn't the Wolf's normal profile. Yes, she matched the look but having a girl that could defend herself...? Very risky.

"One more thing, John," said Jacob fumbling with his notes... Toxicology reports indicate high levels of succinylcholine."

"SUX," John said.

"Let's put it this way, with that much in your body you would never regain nerve use, let alone speak."

"Did we not pick this up in the other bodies?" John said.

"No, nothing," said Jacob.

"Would a victim be able to lash out or run just after taking it?" John said.

"Perhaps for a second, but it would be a second, John... no marathons here," Jacob said.

There was a small pause as John thought for a moment

"What about the prints you pulled from the scene?" John said

"Ah yes, we are checking our system now and working on a

match," Jacob said, turning the pages in his file to find the notes on the print

"If anything comes up on that let me know," said Jacob.

17

John stood outside the infirmary main doors, his back to the wall and leaning against the cold bricks. He had opened his coat to let some air to his body, his shirt had a few buttons open and he rubbed at his eyes. The gum in his mouth was dry. John pulled out the gum and threw it into the bin next to him. The smoke from two men in white hospital gowns bellowed into the cold air. It was 1 pm and the time had flown. It seemed to stop dead when you walked into that hell hole, then realign and start beating again the moment you were set free. John looked at the smokers and wondered if they knew their fate; would he be passing them on one of those silver trolleys on the corridor, or perhaps reading a name tag hanging on a toe? *Shit, who knows?* John thought.

Over the road was a small shopping centre, the glass of its designer walls sparkling. It wrapped around the imposing building like a silver coat. Two window cleaners stood on the path with extended poles prodding and pressing their wet sponges against the silver surface. The frothy water spilled to the street. John and Claire had visited this centre many times. It had some really quirky shops on the first floor that Claire loved. John spent many Saturday mornings being dragged around that place. John remembered there was a nice coffee shop on the ground floor.

"Fuck it, I'll head over," John said to himself, pulling himself from the cold brick wall of the hospital and heading over the road.

The traffic in Leicester centre was chaos; didn't matter what time of day it is, there seemed to be hundreds of cars of different sizes darting around. Fumes bellowed into the sky. People inside stuck to those damn steering wheels, with glazed and angry looks. You took your life into your own hands crossing there, but John couldn't be bothered to walk down the road to the crossing. He preferred the direct route.

John got to the cafe and ordered a latte: small with extra milk, it was better than normal coffee. The girl behind the checkout smiled at John, that fake smile that you know they put on, time and time again... where inside they are fed up as hell. Fake... rehearsed... The combination of different drinks line the walls, some sort of cold coffee iced things John had never heard of. John scanned the different titles... cold iced tea... chia latte... what the hell? John stood, his hands in his pockets, and waited patiently. His head was heavy from the morning's work. He thought he may have looked withdrawn but his mind said; *Excuse me I've just been and looked at a dead girl with her head decapitated, forgive me if I look shit!*

"Will that be all, sir?" the girl said from behind the till, placing the hot latte in front of John in a posh-looking glass cup, and breaking him from his thoughts.

"Ah... yes... yes, that's it, thanks," John said, digging into his pockets and pulling out a note.

Job swap – *What a great idea; tell you what, I'll pour the coffee, you solve the case... don't think the pinny and fake smile would suit me... J*

The cafe had changed since John was in last. It was over eight months ago, when John and Claire visited town. John was happier then and more alive. The staff were different as well. He remembered it was a thin school boy with a spotty face... John remembered asking him if he had ID for a joke...

John sat at the table near the window that looked out into the mall, the jingle of the cafe door, opening and shutting as customers strolled in and out, rang in the air, and the hustle and bustle of the staff pressing at the coffee machines causing the steam to bellow out could be heard. Good place to people watch, but not to think. John sat on the hard wooden chair, rested his elbows on the table and let out a sigh. He rubbed his eyes and took off his coat. He placed his coat on the back of the chair and gently rolled up his sleeves. It was hot in the cafe. John put his phone, ID and evidence bag with the chain in on the table. He sat sipping at his latte and looking at the bag with the gold chain in. He looked hard, trying to understand what he may have missed.

He then had an image in his mind of Claire...

"Look, John, look how nice it is, can't believe it, what a nice gift," Claire said to John.

"Well, they must appreciate you," John said, looking at the gold bracelet on her arm.

John jumped back into reality. He looked up, staring into space.

"That's it, that's it, I knew I had seen that before!" John said to himself.

John remembered six weeks before Claire's death, a new teacher had started... she was young, athletic and was hired to teach PE – MISS PETERS! Shit... it was her! John couldn't believe what he had remembered. She had given Claire a bracelet, a gold bracelet saying 'Best Friend'. She had a neck chain with the same markings... they were close as hell...

John couldn't believe what he was thinking. He covered his eyes and held tightly to the evidence bag in front of him. He grabbed his phone off the table and started scrolling through the pictures. *Where is it? I fucking know it's here... come on...*

"Jesus," John said out loud.

On picture nine was the school photo Claire had sent him; as clear as day standing near Claire in pink top and black trousers, was Carole Peters...

"My God," John said.

John got back to the office at 3 pm. The team had been busy piecing together the evidence and info they had, the whiteboard on the wall covered in names and information. John walked in, threw his coat over the arm of the chair, rolled up his sleeves again and stood in front of the board.

"Right, guys, listen in; this chain… this bloody chain, it was the same Claire had on her wrist, the same damn chain," John said holding up the evidence bag so they could all see.

"Wren, I emailed you a picture; pull it up, please," John said.

"Chloe, pull the blinds," John said.

Chloe pulled down the blinds putting the office in semi-darkness and the projector that always stayed on the table near the sofa was switched on. Wren went over with her laptop and plugged the lead into the projector.

"One minute, sir, it's just loading," Wren said.

"I knew the other day, the moment I saw the chain, hung over the victim's neck, something wasn't right. It was a mark… a sign…" said John.

"A sign for what?" Clive said looking at John.

"Wren, the projector… Jesus… do you know what you're doing?" John said in an impatient way.

"Okay… okay… right, it's ready," said Wren.

The projector burst into life, the picture of the school year large and proud on the wall behind John. John put the bag down and pulled at the fold-up whiteboard on the ceiling.

"What's up with this bleeding thing? Come on, damn you."

With a bang and puff of dust, it rolled down.

The contractors had moved it to install the new lighting and they must have jammed it. It always worked okay before, John thought. The team did their best not to laugh and hid their grins.

"I'll have them when I see them," John said still rolling the whiteboard down.

The picture from the projector shone bright at the crisp

101

whiteboard. John stood to one side admiring the scene, with his face back to normal now after the image had moved to the whiteboard rather than John's face.

"Come on, for God's sake, am I the only one here who can see this?" John said lifting his hands in disbelief as the team sat quietly, looking deeply at the picture in front of them, their pens tapping at their pads.

The team got up and came closer to the image like slow grazing cattle approaching a farmer's feeding bucket.

"I don't believe it," said Wren as she stared at the picture in front of her. "It's Carole and Claire!" she said again.

"This picture was taken at Imperial six weeks before Claire's death, six weeks! They were at the same school. Ladies and gentlemen, we have our connection," John said, pointing at the whiteboard with an excited tone about him knowing a piece of the complex puzzle had fallen into place.

The room fell silent. You could have heard a pin drop… Wren, Chloe, Clive and John all stared at the picture.

The chief walked in just at that moment breaking the silence as the office door screeched open.

"John, any news… any links?" she said.

John looked over at the chief standing in the doorway with her hands on her hips, her suit tight against her trim and tidy frame.

"Yes, ma'am," said John. "Seems our victim knew Claire, ma'am," said John, pointing at the whiteboard.

"What?" said the chief.

"Look for yourself," said John.

The chief walked over to the whiteboard and looked at the picture. She looked carefully at all the images in front of her.

"My God," she said.

"Vendetta?" she said looking at John.

"Looks that way considering it's two people linked to me," John said, shrugging his shoulders.

"Can I see you outside, John?" the chief said as she headed for the office door. John looked at her leaving and followed her with his gaze.

"Wren, prepare the post-mortem shots please," John said as he headed after the chief.

"Yes, sir," Wren said.

John got into the corridor and went straight to the water dispenser, he pulled a cup and starting filling it with water. His back was to the chief as she leant against the wall behind him.

"John, are you okay with this? I mean... it's close for comfort, isn't it?" she said in a soft voice.

"Mary, don't give me the 'can't cope' speech; we went through that last year," John said, still filling the cup.

"I just don't want you getting drawn into something you can't handle, John," she said in a caring manner. "Even I have a boss to report to, John, and he thinks you're too close to this as it is with Claire's death," she said.

"Don't give me that spiel, Mary, you know I'm good at my job. I've worked my ass off with the case. I know they think I've lost the plot... you know me... there hasn't been a drop of shit to work to, nothing... I uncovered every stone... hell, it was my wife, Mary... I tried everything to catch the bastard," John said, his back still to Mary.

"Ahh shit... now look..." John said as the cup overflowed and the water hit his shoes.

Mary put her hand on John's shoulder and came closer.

"I just don't want you to be in too deep, that's all. If it gets too much you'll tell me, won't you, John?" she said. "John, you'll tell me, right?" she said again, rubbing his shoe with a small piece of tissue.

"Yes, yes, yes, I'll tell you," John said looking down at the water on his shoe and the chief bending in her tight dress gently wiping it away.

"Perhaps now you'll buy some new ones, John, rather than these old tatty things," she said, smiling, as she lifted herself up, chucked the tissue in the small silver bin, adjusted her dress, and walked away.

John stood with the cup of water in one hand, watching Mary leave the corridor.

At that point, John's phone rang...

"Jacob, what can I do for you?" John said, holding the cup of water in one hand and his phone in the other, still watching Mary exit the space.

"I've sent the full report over to Wren on email, full findings and toxicology. The DNA from the hair sample is also in there," said Jacob.

"Great... good... fantastic," John said as he tipped the dregs of water from his cup into the cheese plant.

"The shoe print is consistant with hunting boots, the brand pulled on the prints indicate hunting boots as well. Im sure there are not many shops round here that stock these. Size 14 – large feet! They are for deep wooded areas, thick soles, extra warm padding. I'll send you a screenshot of what I mean. They also match one of the site prints found near the other victims," Jacob finished.

"What?" said John in a shocked manor

"It looks to be the same print, John," said Jacob

"Are you sure?" said John

"Hey, that's your job to double check, but my guess is, it's the same guy," said Jacob with a happy tone about him.

John was taking in what Jacob had said.

"One more thing, John... try to keep contamination down to a minimum, there's a good boy," said Jacob in a sarcastic manner. "What?" said John as he walked back into the office.

"What you moaning on about, Jacob?" John said.

"Your DNA, all over the hair sample... wear gloves in the future, big man." Jacob hung up the phone and John stood puzzled. He took a breath, shook his head and let Jacob's words wash over him. He put his phone back into his pocket.

Total bullshit, he thought. *Cheeky twat...*

The information on the prints flowed around John's head...

18

The office was still busy with the team going over the different pictures of Carole from forensics. They were clear shots of the scene, every little detail; the small marker flags standing clear in the gravelled ground of the car park. Wren, Clive and Chloe all fixed on the shots, the sound of pens touching paper as Chloe and Clive noted what they saw. The information on the print pinned neatly on the board.

"Can somebody sort the damn heat in here?" John said as he barged into the office, rolling his sleeves back up as they had dropped from the episode in the corridor.

"Spring, and we are cooking like rabbits!" John pronounced again.

Chloe stood up and placed her pen and pad on the sofa. She headed to the window and lifted a section of the blinds and pushed open two of the large windows. The blind sat awkwardly on her back, pressing her lower to the windowsill; no one got up to help.

"There," she announced pulling herself back out and straightening her attire.

"The necklace: I want to know who, where and when this was purchased. Dig, people, dig," John said, fiddling with his collar.

"The boots that were worn, find out what shops stock these. Find the locations. Use the picture Jacob is sending over. There can't be many shops stocking these.

"Where do we start, sir?" said Clive in a bemused manner.

There was a pause… Clive, Wren and Chloe waited.

"Start at the shopping centre in the city, over the road from the hospital. I'm sure there is a small jewellery shop in there," said John, looking at the whiteboard with the school photo bright as day, and Claire's happy face jumping out at him. "Im sure there are boot shops in there as well. Check the small villages around the city, those small side street shops that sell these special products. Trace the brand!"

"I want to know when Carole purchased this chain, was Claire with her and do they have CCTV?" John had his finger pointed to Carole's picture on the whiteboard tapping it as he made his point.

"What will this tell us though, sir?" said Wren.

"It will give us a starting point. We have a connection between Claire and Carole, not just a chain or arm bracelet, but a workplace… there is a link. This isn't a coincidence… the Wolf plans things carefully," John said. "We need to check detail."

"We have a chain, boot prints… come on people, this is what we have been waiting for," said John

John held his emotion well but it was hell for him with the picture of Claire pinned to the whiteboard in front of him; shots of her body, the bin, the toe tag from the mortuary… torture. It took a great man to hold that type of deep emotion, bottle it and keep it from fizzing out of the top. John did it to perfection.

Clive had moved from his chair to his computer.

"Sir, I've got the latest on the CCTV images," Clive said, looking deep at the screen.

"Okay, what do we have?" John said walking over.

"Sir, do you want a tea?" Wren said as he walked by.

"Yes, good idea. Need something to keep my eyes open," John said.

Wren lifted up and headed out into the hall. Chloe was still sat looking at the images in front of her; they were changing from one to another on a loop. Wren was good with technology. She could do things with computers and phones that John thought was magic… well above his knowledge.

"We have an image of a van that matches the description from our witness. Camper, dark in colour, can't see the plates but windows look blacked out," said Clive. "Same van here."

"Times?" said John.

"First one is heading north into the city at 11 pm, next is heading west at 3 pm, sir."

"Where is the park positioned in connection to this image?" John said, pointing at the screen.

"The park is west side of the canal, sir, so it's the right direction," Clive said.

"What's that?" John pointed at the screen and touched the monitor. The monitor went black.

"Shit… what? I only touched the damn thing with my finger!" John said with a confused look on his face.

At that point, Wren walked in with a tray of coffee, tea and some sandwiches. She had to open the office door with her bum as the tray took up both of her hands, the receipt pressed between her teeth. She came over and put the tray on the small table in front of the sofa, the images from the projector lighting up her face and Chloe looking at John and Clive. John and Clive were muttering and arms were flapping.

"Coffee, guys," Wren said, breaking John and Clive's state. "Can't believe how much this costs. I'm sure they have a different charge for us than the rest. They always have big smiles on their faces the moment I get to the till. One day I'm going to chuck a bucket of ice cold water over them just for fun," Wren said handing out the coffee and sandwiches.

"Just give me the receipts and I'll sort it," John said.

"Ah… that reminds me, sir, can you sign my overtime sheet?" Clive said.

"Jesus, Clive… you pick your moments," John said just

picking up his tea with the number two written on the side (indicating two sugars), bending his large frame nearer the table.

Clive muttered and grabbed at his coffee. Wren and Chloe looked at him and giggled. John wasn't one for signing things; it took him all his time to sign Grey's card. It was as if signing things made him vulnerable. Who knew? He was shit at it. The guys in his team knew they had to remind him at least seven times per month; that way they stood a chance of getting expenses signed off in time for pay day.

"Wren, sort Clive's damn machine, will you? Crap thing went black on us," John said, sipping at his tea and holding a cheese and onion sandwich.

Wren walked over to Clive's desk and with less than five seconds the monitor jumped back into life.

"There," she announced.

"What do you mean 'there'?" said John.

"You had pressed the off switch, bottom left..." Wren said pointing at the button.

"Next time, Clive, be more careful," John said with a small smile.

The images of the van were on several shots from different cameras, each time a piece of a different part. One camera the back, one the side, the other the windows. One thing was clear, it matched Sophie's description. You could make out a blackening to the side windows as Sophie described but the black and white images made it hard.

"Isn't there any way this can be cleaned up?" John said, keeping his hands wrapped round his tea and this time avoiding touching the screen.

"This is straight from tec, sir. It is cleaned up," Clive said.

"Shit... okay. The black windows that we assume match what Sophie said; do we think it could be film? A kind of self-stuck item?" John said.

"You mean the type of stuff from one of those car parts shops?" Wren said.

"Yes, that's it, you can see small creases to its colour. Looks like bubbles almost," John said.

"Could he have stuck this on himself, but pissed the job up?" John said again, still looking at the screen.

"Possible," said Clive, "but we will never be able to trace that. Even if he had a shop do it for him, there are numerous around Leicester. There are even private companies who do it," said Clive.

John and Wren nodded at his points.

"Okay, we have a van near the scene, and the times sort of fit... we don't have a face or plates... we have no other witnesses," John said, holding his cup and tapping at the desk.

"It tells us that we have a camper, in Leicestershire... old style, blacked windows... Someone must have seen this vehicle," said John.

"Wren, call Sophie and ask her to tell us the colour. I don't even think we asked this," said John.

"Red," said Wren.

"What?" said John.

"The colour of the camper was red," said Wren reading from her notes...

John smiled and looked at Wren.

"Good job, we have a red camper 1950 – 1970 in age, blacked-out windows, driving late at night... we have something. I would know that style anywhere," said John.

"How would you know that style, sir? You a camper anorak?" said Chloe, still sat on the sofa.

"My dad had one for years. He used to pick me and Mark up from school in it... shitty thing but he kept it pristine. I think after the TV, it was the only other thing he loved. He got rid after Mark disappeared," said John.

The room fell silent. The guys listened to John's words but had no comments. It was hard when John mentioned Mark.

"I'll keep on the CCTV, sir," said Clive. "Perhaps we can get some more."

"Check petrol stations; he must have stopped to fuel up somewhere. Check the vicinity of the scene, check a radius of say ten miles and work your way in. Let's see what hits we get," John said finishing his tea and starting on his sandwich.

"There can't be too many of that style van in Leicestershire," said John.

Chloe had looked at all the images. She surveyed them making sure they had every detail. She switched the projector off and walked over to her desk.

"Sir, meant to tell you, the Peters are identifying the body tomorrow. They called in earlier. Eleven o'clock, I think it was."

"Right," said John. "Call them, Chloe, and ask if we can see them afterwards at their house, say 1 pm."

John headed into his small office with his sandwich and sat at his desk, he leaned back in his seat and bit at the white bread in front of him. He sat in concentration, Clive, Chloe and Wren busy in the office outside. He sat going over every detail piece by piece: Carole's body; the park; the cuts; the van; the necklace; prints. He placed the bits of the puzzle in different boxes in his mind. The picture of him and Claire sat looking at him on his desk. John raised a small smile. The picture was from their honeymoon in Corfu. They spent two weeks in the sun. It was very hot and John was bitten to fuck... but it was worth it. They stayed in a villa in a village called Nissaki, which was quiet and peaceful. John's phone rang now and again; two more deaths during that period from the Wolf. Work and pleasure always somehow combined in a circle of shit. Claire on the other hand was completely free. John remembered the times he spent just watching her lie on the sunbed, the hot Greek sun belting down on her back, the tiny sweat droplets glittering in the sun. A scene of pure pleasure. Those were good times.

John opened the desk and pulled out a small picture without

a frame. It was a picture of Claire in front of a taverna. She was dressed perfectly, just like a model. Her long dark hair and tanned features, her pink sunglasses; everything was right. This was the taverna they visited every night. John rubbed at the picture as if running his fingers through Claire's hair. He sniffed out his nose and let out a sigh. *Why the fuck her? It should have been someone else. Why her?* he thought.

John hadn't been back to Corfu since; he did think about it during his leave, but dismissed it in his mind. Too many memories…

At that point, Wren knocked on the glass on John's door. She saw him holding the photo in one hand and a half-eaten cheese sandwich in the other. She watched him for a moment from the door knowing he was someplace else in his mind… she knew how hard it had been for him over the last year. How he held it together… she would never know.

"Sir, sorry to disturb you but just to let you know the results from Jacob have landed and I'll get straight on them, in the morning. I've got to head off. It's my friend's big birthday: drink… sex… you know… messy…"

"Sex… yes… yes… know what you mean," John said, still holding and looking at the photo. He wasn't really listening to what Wren was saying, the cheese sandwich was still in his hand and his mouth was half open ready to take a bite, but the sandwich never quite made it.

"I'll see you in the morning. I've emailed the file over to you as well," said Wren, knowing he was still in a daze.

"Yes… right… night, Wren… night," said John breaking from his thoughts and looking at his watch. It was 6 pm. He finished the sandwich, pushing it fully into his mouth, and threw the wrapper in his bin. The bin was overflowing with paper and crap.

"Do you need a lift?" said Wren still standing at the door.

"No, I'm good. Tell the guys to head off; don't want Clive

getting cramp from writing down more overtime hours!" said John with a smile, placing the picture back in the drawer and shutting it closed with a clunk.

The office was silent at night, like a cemetery, John thought. There were small rattles from the radiators and the faint buzz from the fridge in the corner. The shadows darted round the room as the traffic outside lit up the space. The blinds were fully up and the windows closed. The team had settled the room for the night and only three of the LED lights were on, creating a white glow that lit patches throughout the office. It looked like lights from a spacecraft. The computers on the desks settled into sleep mode. John sat at his desk and pulled a small bottle of whisky from his bottom drawer. A glass also sat near the bottle in preparation. He poured a small glass and sat back in his chair with his eyes closed. It had been a hell of a few days. The light from his monitor lit his face. The email from Wren sat clearly in his inbox. John rolled down his sleeves and opened a few more buttons. The peace and quiet danced in his mind...

"John, what the hell are you still doing here? It's late," said Mary, looking in at him from his office door.

"Jesus, Mary, you scared the hell out of me," John said, jumping forward in his chair and nearly spilling the glass of whisky.

"You should be home; too many memories, John," she said leaning against the door frame. Her curvy frame and handbag formed an image to John of a call girl waiting for business. Her image was dark and sexual in the fading light of the office. Her long hair hung gracefully each side of her head.

"You know me, Mary, I get lost in my thoughts!" John said, taking a sip of his drink and calming his beating heart. *Easy, John... easy*, he thought.

Mary looked at John. She liked him... really liked him. His dark complexion, his long hair... the way he wore his shirts; it made her quiver inside. She admired how much of a damn good cop he was. Mary found him very sexy. She made gentle comments but trod carefully; she knew Claire was the love of John's life. The ring he still wore, proof of his devotion. Her position at the force also made it difficult.

"You fancy a drink, John?" Mary said, still standing in her pose.

John looked at Mary and gently placed his glass on the table. He took a moment to think about what she was asking then a voice inside him said:

Go on, John... go on... a drink won't hurt... you deserve some fun... go on...

It was Claire, clear as day. It was the approval John needed.

"Ok, why not?" John grabbed his coat which was hanging over the back of his seat, stood up and tidied himself. He pushed his hair back and smiled at Mary. They both walked out of the office, switching the last of the lights off on their way. The picture of John and Claire on his desk was lit up from the lights outside. Claire, smiling in the shot. Approval...

19

John's doorbell rang, giving out its normal 'ding dong', vibrating through John's living room and kitchen. John was up, and already had the house blinds open, light and airy. The early morning sun beat through the windows. John wore his normal attire: his black jeans, leather suede shoes, clean blue shirt and black coat. John had been through the same routine this morning as normal and he had taken his pills. The table in the front room was clear, all the magazines had been removed and the glasses cleared. The room looked fresh. John had got back round eleven. Mary had kept him chatting in a small pub around the corner from the office. It was a pub that seemed to just fill with cops; although they were not in uniform, a cop knows a cop. John and Mary had sat in a small window seat near the open fire. The pub was dated but cosy. They talked about normal things away from work. It was the first time since Claire had passed away that John felt human again.

'Ding dong'… the doorbell rang again.

It was 8 am and Wren was outside waiting, her small frame only covering half the coloured glass in John's door, the light seeping through just enough above Wren's head. John opened the door and without looking said,

"Morning, Wren, how's the head?"

"How can you be sure it's me? You don't even look… I mean,

it could be anyone. The head is fine, thanks," Wren said, moving forward into John's home.

"It's not the fact that I just assume, Wren. Oh no," said John, checking himself in his mirror in the living room and tidying his hair. "It's the fact that your small torso covers only certain sections of the glass in my door; the light that remains and shines through makes a shape that is only recognisable as you!" John said, smiling. "I can't mistake that halo anywhere, and this morning the beer smell, that also helped!" John said.

"Good morning to you too, sir!" Wren said, smiling back.

Wren was in her normal attire and the Audi had somehow managed to squeeze its way directly in front of John's house. Maybe the late night had helped. Who knows? John looked past Wren, still adjusting his shirt in the mirror and said, "I hope you didn't lift the car out as you threatened."

"No, sir, although I was tempted," Wren said, smiling.

"Shame," said John. "I'm sure that the sound would have made them run out from that glass monster at the back!" John said in a sarcastic manner, referring to the neighbour's extension.

Fuckers, he said in his mind.

John and Wren hit the road. It was 9.30 am by the time they had made their way over the city to Mr and Mrs Peters house in Fleckney, it was nearly 1 pm. They had made numerous stops before and the morning seemed to go nowhere. It was a street called Park View, named because a small, quaint park sat over the road. Its small green fence wrapped round it, the sound of the large trees rustling in the morning wind. The sun was high in the sky and it was a stunning day. It had rained on and off during the night, and also early morning. Some of the lower branches on the trees hung low from the weight of the water. The road was still wet. Wren's Audi turned into the road. It was tree-lined and quiet. There were cars parked to one side only and the 'No Parking' signs littered the other. The houses were a mixture of Victorian villas and terrace.

"Number twelve, sir, I believe," Wren said looking at her phone.

"I wish you wouldn't do that, Wren... concentrate on the road or pull over," John said sitting next to her and beginning to sweat.

The Audi came to a stop outside number twelve. It was a Victorian terrace; like a terrace house but larger, with posher windows. The wood on the windows was painted and sealed, and a small garden in front was bursting with life. The rectangular herringbone tiles led to the inset Victorian stained door. *Right up my street,* John thought.

"We need to play this carefully, Wren. Remember, they identified Carole this morning. Best behaviour," John said, getting out of the car and straightening himself up, his ID at the ready and the gum he was chewing on the way, disposed of into its wrapper.

The small picket gate opened softly against its latches. You could tell the house was cared for and in good order... if first impressions counted, John knew they were an upper-class family and appearance was key. He recalled his old street when he lived at home and how the curtains twitched and moved, every little detail of each house somehow known by all. Your neighbour knew what was happening to you before you did... Jenny always joked about this. John made the comparisons in his mind, keeping his expression plain.

Wren and John stood at the door; Wren pressed the bell and, similar to John's, it let out a 'Ding dong'.

John looked to his left and spotted a figure at the window in his sixties. He had silver hair and glasses and was gazing at them both as they stood there looking out of place for the neighbourhood. John aimed his ID at the window and mouthed police with no sound. The man nodded and edged away from the window. A few moments later the door opened.

"Mr Peters, I presume?" John said in a soft tone.

"Yes, that's me," said the grey-haired man in front of John.

"I'm DI Miste and this is DS Walker. We are from the serious crime unit and would like to know if it's okay to come in for a chat?" John said again in a soft voice but holding out his ID in his left hand. Wren was doing the same. Mr Peters looked at the ID then looked at them both, taking in the scene. He looked closely over his glasses at them... the dark bags under his eyes and the creased polo shirt said a lot to John. He leant on a cane, but looked fit for his age. The cane did not match his demeanour.

"We are really sorry to trouble you at this difficult time," John said placing his ID back in his jacket, "but we need a chat about Carole."

"You don't look like police. They told us the police would be round today for a statement; they told us to expect two officers?" the man said, looking up and down at John and Wren.

"We are detectives, sir; we are working on this case as part of our unit," John said.

Mr Peters looked at John for a moment then looked at Wren.

"I recognise you, Miste, I recognise you from the papers. Yes, last year if my mind tells me right. What was it? Something about a woman... yes."

John butted in. "Sir, can we come in? It's important we have a chat," John said in a more prominent voice.

"Yes, yes, come in, come in." Mr Peters waved them into the hall. He looked from left to right outside the door before he came back in wobbling on his cane and closed the door behind him.

"You okay, Mr Peters?" Wren said, steadying him in the hall.

"Oh im fine, after the morning we have had... I'm fine. I don't need a young whippersnapper helping me, thank you," Mr Peters said, pulling himself away from Wren.

"Damn neighbours, nosy sods... nothing to do with them. Amazing, isn't it? Already had a sympathy card yesterday... I mean, already? How the hell did they know already? Damn busybodies..." said Mr Peters, walking deeper into the hall, the herringbone tile tapping under his walking stick.

John smiled recalling his earlier thoughts. *Yep, that's right... bastards... know before you do*, he thought.

"In there, please, I'll get my wife," said Mr Peters, pointing into the front room.

John and Wren walked into the front room. The ceiling was large and light. There was a huge chandelier hanging in the centre with what must have been a thousand light bulbs on it, John thought. A marble fireplace stood proud in the centre with a log burner in the middle, the charred remains of the wood still sitting inside. A basket with one log remaining sat to the right, and a gold poker to the left.

The floor was red tiled, not carpeted. The furnishings were dated and they had that smell of times past. An ashtray sat on the small glass table in front of the sofa, a small brown cigar still smoking away. The armchair in the window was dented from the force of Mr Peters. It was an old leather thing with green arms.

John and Wren sat on the sofa looking round the room. They could hear Mr Peters in the kitchen and the faint noise of water and glasses being washed. The smell of perfume filled the air from an air freshener spitting out its contents every time it sensed a movement.

"This is my wife, Lynsey," said Mr Peters, standing at the door on his cane, with a small grey-haired lady beside him. She was wearing an apron and yellow gloves, her hair was tied back and her face gaunt. Her face was that of a rabbit in a car's headlights; John knew the expression well. It's when you're stuck in some sort of time and space between reality, everything around you colliding but nothing making sense. And there's you, floating in the middle of all this shit... you could be anywhere... just not here at that moment. The morning must have been hell, and to see their daughter in the way she was, shit!

John stood.

"Mrs Peters, I'm DI Miste and this is DS Walker. We are here bec—" John's speech was interrupted.

"Tea… coffee… biscuit?" Lynsey said breaking John's rhythm.

John paused for a moment, the question thowing him from his speech.

"Yes… yes, that would be nice, thank you…" said John gently, sitting back on the sofa.

"Thank you, Mrs Peters," said Wren.

"Call me Lynsey," she said rushing off to make the tea. You could hear the clattering in the background as she busied herself.

"She isn't coping," Mr Peters said quietly, shaking his head. "She says she is… but she isn't," he said again. "I don't know what's worse, the not knowing or the knowing," he said fumbling his way to his chair and slamming down into it with a thump.

"It's a very difficult time for you and we are sorry to do this," John said.

"Sorry?" Mr Peters said. "Sorry?

We called you and told you she was missing. All we got was 'we will look into it' from some daft tart at reception. Crap… total crap," Mr Peters said with a raised voice, pointing his finger directly at John. "And this… well, your fault as well," he said pointing at his foot. "Rushing around, running after her… damn near killed myself on the stairs," he said again.

"All your fault!" he said sitting back in his chair and taking a breath. Making us do that this morning, now sit through more crap the same day! Total shit, he said again.

John was used to this and had taken this beating many times. He knew to sit back and take it… take in what they were saying… and nod.

"All I can do is apologise, Mr Peters. We are sorry it has come to this but you have to understand, we deal with hundreds of missing people's cases per week. Most of them turn up a few weeks later. Very few lead to this," John said, his hands on his knees, speaking calmly.

"Yes, well… crap… tax payer's money… rubbish," said Mr Peters settling back after his dig.

Lynsey walked in with a small tray covered in flowers, her smile beaming over her face, her yellow gloves removed and her white skin and purple veins standing proud on her hands. She had a very soft way about her; different to her husband; broken inside. She put the tray on the small table and sat in the chair to the opposite side of her husband.

John thought this strange as it was at times like this where you needed each other. You could have cut the atmosphere with a knife. Perhaps it was the effects of the morning settling in her mind.

"Please… please, take a drink!" she said, pointing at the tray in front of John and Wren.

"Sugar and biscuits, help yourself," she said again.

"Thank you, Mrs Peters," said John as he lent forward and took one of the small china teacups and added two lumps of sugar from the pot. Wren took the other; no sugar, just a tad of milk.

They both sat back and took a sip at the tea. Mr and Mrs Peters sat either end, staring at each other as if facing each other for a fight.

John spotted this and looked at them both, as if readying to stop a fight.

"I'm sorry to have to do this to you both, I really am, especially under the circumstances, but we need to know as much as we can about your daughter. The full details," John said taking a small biscuit from the tray and placing it in his mouth. The china cup sat balancing on his knee.

"Well, what do you want to know? You must have read the report we filed about her when we reported her missing. God, that had all the detail," Mr Peters said raising his arms.

"Norman, it's all right," said Lynsey.

"On the day that you reported your daughter missing, what made you do this? I mean, what triggered it?" John said.

"She hadn't turned up for work and that was unusual for her," said Lynsey.

"We all get up on the dot at 6 am sharp, always have, always will," said Mr Peters in his blank manor.

"Settle yourself down, you'll pull a muscle," said Lynsey, pointing at him to sit back in his seat.

"On that morning she left for work, was there anything unusual; the way she acted, her normal routine... anything?" said John taking another bite at the biscuit.

"Nice, aren't they?" Lynsey said, pointing at the biscuit in John's hand.

"Yes Lynsey, they are. Remind me of the ones my mum used to make. Tried myself once but I haven't got the golden touch," John said, smiling at her. This put Lynsey at ease and a calm smile came over her face.

"You're not like the others; you're different," she said, looking at John and placing her hand on his knee. "You'll find who did this, won't you? I mean, you'll find him, yes?" she asked.

John leaned forward and put his cup on the small tray on the table. He wiped his mouth with the back of his hands and the crumbs fell in his lap. Wren watched and gently sipped her tea.

"I promise you, Lynsey, I won't stop until I have who did this. Never," he said placing his hand on top of hers.

"Two murders in one year... bleeding joke... absolute joke. You didn't find who killed her friend, did you? No, another case left open," said Norman.

"I beg your pardon?" said John.

"The other woman, last year at her school... damn tragedy... two girls from the same school, and two close to us," he said again.

"Are you talking about Claire?" Wren said looking at Norman carefully as he sat in his chair shaking his head.

"Yes, that was her... Claire... very nice lady, she came here once or twice... bloody nice lady. She had a fellow, always spoke highly of him..."

John sat quietly taking in what he was being told. He didn't say a word, just listened, his mind jumping from left to right. He thought about Claire walking in the house, he thought of her maybe even sitting on this very sofa. Christ... he took a deep breath.

"The morning Carole left, was there anything?" he said again, repeating his earlier question.

"She got up with us, normal morning routine, then picked up her things and left for the school."

"Did she drive or catch the bus?" Wren said.

"She caught the bus," said Norman. "Her car is on the front, see!" he said pointing his cane at the window like an arrow

"Would you mind if DS Walker looked round it, please?" John said.

"No... no, not at all, the keys are on the table in the hall," said Norman.

Wren got up and walked into the hall. The keys were sitting on a small table in the hall just as he had said. They had a large, soft charm attached. Wren took the keys and went outside. She shut the door behind her.

"What time did the school call you and tell you she hadn't got there?" John said.

"Around 9.30 am. It was the head teacher. Norman answered the phone," said Lynsey. "Norman, what did she say to you?" Lynsey asked, raising her voice so her husband took note.

"Nothing much... just she hadn't turned up... and was she

ill. I said she left normal time and as far as we were aware she had gone to work."

"That was it?" John said.

"Yes, what did you expect…? We are not bleeding psychic, Miste!" Norman said, using John's last name and a raised voice. It reminded him of school, the way the teachers used to call him to the front to read out his homework to the class.

"We thought she had perhaps met her boyfriend, or even that the bus was late!" said Lynsey.

"Boyfriend?" said John.

"Yes, Nathan," said Lynsey.

"And how long has she been seeing Nathan?" John asked.

"About six weeks, I would say," Lynsey said smiling at John. "Have some more tea if you like, plenty to go round," she said refilling John's cup from the teapot in the centre.

"Thank you, Lynsey," John said.

"Aren't you going to write anything down, Miste?" Norman said.

"I don't need to, Norman. I have a kind of… photo mind I think it's called… I always tend to remember the details," John said, sipping at his second cup of tea.

John had a mind of a computer. From his early days at school through to his days on the force, the detail would stick. His persona didn't reflect his intelligence. Pictures and information would be placed in parts of his mind and he could pick at them whenever he needed. He didn't know how but he just could.

"How did Carole and Nathan meet?" John asked.

"One of those online dating things," Lynsey said.

"She was a quiet one, our Carole… never had many boyfriends or anything like that, kept to herself and was career-minded. Takes after her dad, I'm afraid," said Lynsey pointing at her husband. "House doesn't seem the same without her. The light has gone," she said.

"Does that make sense, Detective? It feels dark!" she said looking at John deeply.

"How can he know? He hasn't lost someone like we have," Norman said.

"I know your pain, Lynsey, trust me I do," John said.

"Know our pain! After what we had to see this morning, I don't think so, Mister!" said Norman sharply.

Wren was outside looking round the car. It was a bright red Beetle, silver wheels. The old-fashioned type, not the new sort. Wren pulled her blue gloves from her pocket, put them on and opened the car door. The driver's door was to the path. The car was very clean, an umbrella sat on the back seat and a large set of pink dice hung on the driver's mirror. The interior was red and white leather, very retro. Wren checked the door pockets and glovebox. The glovebox light jumped to life and lit all the contents inside. There was a stereo face, satnav, cloth, charger and hairbrush. Normal bits. At the back was a receipt. Wren pulled out the receipt and sat back in the car seat. The receipt was from a jeweller in the shopping centre. It was for a gold necklace and bracelet. Both with identification writing.

Wren looked at the receipt and nodded.

"Got you," she said in an excited manner. "£765! Jesus, some gold, some friend..." she said. She placed the receipt in a small evidence bag she had in her pocket and sealed the top.

Wren called the office and arranged a pickup for the car. She didn't want to drive it and disturb any evidence that may be in there. She got out, closed the car door, and took off her gloves. She walked back to the house. She opened the door with the key on the car key set. There was a car key, house key and one more key. It was a house key by the looks of it, but not this one. Wren tried it in the door lock to be sure and it didn't move the lock. It was an old style key, large and worn. A key that had seen some use.

"Can you describe Nathan to me?" John said to Lynsey. "Do you have any photos of him?" he said again.

"We don't have any photos, but Carole may have on her phone. We found it here in her bedroom on the day she went missing," Lynsey said. "I'll get it for you if you want?"

"Yes please," said John.

Lynsey left the room. You could hear her scurrying up the stairs.

"The boyfriend, Mr Peters, can you describe him? I mean, did he come round?"

"We only saw him once. I didn't like the guy; gave me the spooks," Norman said.

"In what way?" John said, now rejoined by Wren.

"He was stocky, short hair... about your height... think he was a mechanic or something... not sure. She said he worked at some sort of garage in town... drove a van. We didn't see him again and it was the first time he had been round."

"A van?" said John. "Can you be more specific?"

"One of those camper vans, retro things!" Lynsey said as she walked back in the room holding the phone out to John.

Its diamond stud case sparkled against the light.

"Thank you, Lynsey. You say camper van? Can you describe it?" John said, his mind in deep concentration.

"Think it was red... silver wheels... I remember the wheels because they were alloy things, not the originals I remember... and the engine... bloody noisy," she said, taking a biscuit from the tray.

"That's right, you could hear the damn thing coming up the street. I mean, what would the neighbours think? Bloody boy racer!"Norman said.

"The one time you saw him, how long ago was this?" John asked.

"Probably about a few days in; he knocked on the door," Norman answered. "I was in the kitchen. By the time I got to the front room he was walking back to the van," he said.

"What was he dressed like?" John said.

"He was dressed in black jeans, boots and T-shirt... too bloody cold for that if you ask me... bloody fool," said Norman.

"You don't think he had anything to do with this, do you?" asked Lynsey.

"We just need to cover all angles, Lynsey, cover all tracks," said John, his hands clasped in a prayer-like state.

"Wren, call Clive. Have him check out the local garages."

"Yes, sir," said Wren, leaving the room with her phone in hand.

"Can you describe the look of Nathan; his face?" said John.

"He looked like that James Bond guy... Daniel something...?" Norman said.

"Daniel Craig?" John said.

"That's him, that look. No earrings, nothing like that. Too cheap for our daughter, you could tell... bleeding mechanic... I mean, come on..." said Norman.

"Your thoughts, Lynsey?" John said looking at Lynsey who had drifted back into one of her trances.

"Mrs Peters?" John said.

"I see her, you know!"

"Pardon?" said John.

"Carole; I see her, you know... from time to time... her smile... her laugh... she calls my name."

"Jesus," said Norman covering his eyes.

"Mrs Peters, we will do everything we can to help, I promise," John said, tapping her hand again. "You've gone through a traumatic experience, especially this morning," said John.

"Is there anything else, Detective? Shouldn't you be out there trying to catch this bastard?" Norman said again.

"Just one more thing. Can I see the room, please?" John said.

"Of course. First door to the left as you walk along the landing," said Lynsey.

"When can we get her home? When can we sort the funeral?" Norman asked.

"In a few days, Mr Peters, we just need a bit more time with her to make sure we have everything we need," John said in a calm voice. "By the way, do you know Nathan's last name?" John said as he left the room.

"I don't go around asking everyone their last name Miste, Jesus…Is this really what we are paying our taxes for!" Norman said shaking his head.

John just stood looking into the air, he couldn't push as he knew the situation was sensitive.

"Which door did you say, Mr Peters?" John asked.

"First door on the left, yes?" Norman said, pointing towards the door from his chair.

"That's right," said Lynsey.

John climbed the stairs.

20

Carole's bedroom was a calming space. The moment John opened the door he felt at peace. It was decorated in a pastel green, the Buddha wall art around the walls matching its feel. She had chimes hanging up at the windows and a large four-poster bed against one wall. Her dresser and wardrobe sat neatly, like in one of those movies where you open a door and it's like time stands still. Her furniture was wood, not wood effect but solid oak. She had a TV and everything she needed to make it her own space. It was clear to John she lived there full-time. John pulled the blue gloves from his pocket and put them on, as well as over shoes to be extra careful. He tucked in his shirt and begin to glide round the room. The dresser was in front of the large Victorian window. It had an old mirror sat on the top that seemed to match the large Victorian sash window. The light flooded in the room and the patterns from the trees outside darted on the bedroom walls. The large silver curtains hanging each side of the window were heavy on their poles. A thick white radiator sat strong and proud just below the windowsill with its silver valves. Not a sign of dust or dirt. John stood in front of the dresser and looked down at its contents. He could hear the beeping of a reverse buzzer outside. John looked over the mirror and down on to the street. The police tow had landed to collect Carole's car to take it to the pound for forensics to work on. Wren was waving and guiding the vehicle into position. She looked like a lollipop lady but without the sign... this thought made John laugh. Mr Peters was out pointing his cane. John couldn't hear him but assumed he was pissing on about the noise and the neighbours... some people just moan all the time!

Carole's dresser was like every woman's in the county: it held all the items she needed for her daily routine. John prodded and lifted them gently with his pen. He opened the drawer to reveal more perfume and odds and ends. As he looked up, some pictures caught his eye. Carole had stuck some photos around her mirror making a collage. John zoomed in on one and took a breath... it was Claire, Carole, and two other teachers on sports day. They were all smiling and wearing wet T-shirts from the fun that day, the yellow buckets in front of them with 'sponsor us' written as clear as day. The kids in the background were jumping and running, stuck in a time warp.

John took the photo off and held it in his hand.

His thumb gently rubbed against Claire's face. It was so close to home for John, seeing this, had hit a nerve. He was holding his emotion with all his strength. *Claire... I miss you so much*, he thought.

"Find anything of interest, Detective?" a voice asked from the door. It was Lynsey.

John turned quickly as if in shock to see someone there.

"No, nothing of any significance," John said, placing the photo into his pocket.

Just as he turned he noticed another photo on its back on top of a small shelf near a large teddy. He went over with concentration on his face and lifted the photo. It was Carole with a man. John looked at it carefully and studied the male.

"Lynsey, do you know this man?" asked John holding the photo out so Lynsey could see.

"No, im sorry," she said.

"Do you think it could be Nathan?" John asked.

"It could be, I never saw him; when he came round I was in the kitchen," said Lynsey

"Problem is it doesn't match your husband's description of him, this guy is tall and thin?" John said, still aiming the photo at Lynsey.

"Sorry, im not sure, it looks like a camper van in the back?" said Lynsey studying the photo.

"It does indeed," said John keeping hold of the photo.

Carole was hand in hand on a bench with the man in the park over the road. You could tell they had used a selfie stick as his hand was stretched lower down the photo, gripping the handle. You could just see the bottom of the stick they used. A camper could be seen in the background past the rallings. John looked around the room and spotted a selfie stick leaning up against the dresser. He walked over and picked it up carefully.

"Do you mind if I take this, Lynsey, for forensics to check?" John said, holding the selfie stick.

"'That's fine, please do as you need," she said.

"I'll need to get forensics in to sweep the room for evidence," John said.

At that point, she began to cry. She walked over and sat on Carole's bed, the tears streaming down her face. She pulled a hanky from her pocket and wiped at her tears.

"I'm sorry... it's just... the emotion... it builds inside... I blame myself. Norman... well, he isn't coping and we have been at each other's throats for a while now. My God, is she really gone?" she said, tears rolling down her face. "This morning was so hard, so hard... I never thought I would ever have to do anything like that, Detective," she said tears dripping in her hands.

John walked over and sat near Lynsey. He put his arms over her shoulders and hugged her. He rubbed up and down her back with the comfort of a parent hugging a child. He closed his eyes. The blue gloves creasing as his hands moved back and forwards.

"It's okay, Mrs Peters, it's okay. It will take time; you've suffered a great loss. You then get us knocking on your door asking all sorts of things. I'm sorry... so sorry for your loss."

"Just catch him, Detective" she said, drying her tears away. "Catch him."

John and Wren left Mr and Mrs Peters' house; Carole's car had been taken to be checked over, and John carried a small, clear evidence bag he had carefully placed the photo in. He had shown Norman the photo on the way out and he confirmed it wasn't the guy who knocked the door. He took his gloves off and rolled them back into his coat pocket. Wren took hers off and did the same. They had been at the property for a few hours and had gone through the motions. John had told the Peters he would be sending forensics around to check Carole's room for prints so to stay out of the room as much as possible. He also told them he would need to take swabs from them to rule their DNA out of the equation. Wren also had the receipt for the gold in an evidence bag in her hand. All in all, it had been a successful day. There was confusion over the Nathan character, but John put this down to the stress. It was 4 pm and the clouds were building in the sky, the once bright sun had faded and the branches of the trees were swinging hard with the wind. Some loose leaves were blowing down the road. John and Wren got to the car and got in. John grabbed the gum from his pocket and placed it in his mouth and took a sigh. The evidence bag sat on his knee, the faces of Carole and a male shining through the clear bag looking straight at John.

"What you thinking?" said Wren. "Sir, what's on your mind?" she said again.

"It's just seeing photos of Claire, brings it all back," said John, scratching his stubbly face.

"You okay?" asked Wren looking at John.

John pulled out the photo from his back pocket and threw it on Wren's lap.

"Where is that from?" Wren said.

"Her room, Blu-tacked on to the mirror."

"You shouldn't have taken it, sir, forensics are due!" Wren said, worried for John.

"Fuck 'em it's my wife," John said. "Drop me back at mine as I want to get my head round all this."

"Can you head back to the office and catch up with Clive and Chloe, see if we have anything more on the camper and the garages in the vicinity? I'll scan the photo over when I get back," John said. "Let's hope they have done their jobs and come up with something for us!"

"Shall I check out the jewellers?" said Wren.

"No, leave that until the morning, but don't give too much away, make out it's routine. We need to clarify this Nathan guy and check the camper van link. We seem to have two different characters with Carole," said John.

"Was she seeing two men?" said Wren.

"She doesn't seem the type, but let's not rule it out," said John.

Wren started the engine and the car rolled out of the street.

21

It was late into the evening by the time John had worked his way through the detail, his small office in the spare bedroom lit only from the desk lamp next to his computer. The clock on the wall ticked through the hours. It was 11 pm. With the pictures and data strewn on his wall, it looked more like the office than a bedroom. John sat in his chair, swaying backwards and forwards in a rocking sensation. He wore shorts and a T-shirt. Comfort clothes... they helped him think and removed him from the normal daily grind. It had been a good day and a shit day, a day of two halves. There was one thing John liked about being a detective: the day flew by and he had no time to think about his own issues. A glass sat on his desk with a small drop of whisky and a plate with the remains of a pasta dish. *Single man's supper*, John would think. The rest of the house sat dark.

The street was quiet, the lamp posts gently glowing a yellow light on to the dark road below. The rain glowed in their glare and gently tapped at the window. The glare of the city in the background was proud against the night sky. John always had the blinds slightly opened; he let the night roll into the room. Somehow, it made him think deeper, a kind of comfort like a warm blanket on a winter night.

John had used string to connect the photos and notes on his wall. The string was corner to corner and all connected to the name 'Wolf' in the middle. The words 'who are you' with a question mark were clear as day, the images and faces of all the victims stuck with blu-tack to the wall. The air was thick with the taste of sorrow. Claire hated this room. She would stay clear, the images of the poor souls glaring at her as she walked in the room, and some were not images she wanted stuck in her mind. She kept a distance from John's work.

John got up from his chair and walked round the room, the glass of whisky in his hand and the glow of the desk lamp bouncing off his white T-shirt. The sound of the rain danced against the car roofs, and a distant fox howling in the air, filled the room.

John's eyes darted round the information: Claire… Carole… the letter… van… chain… the boyfriend… the connection. *I'm connected to Claire, who is connected to Carole… Why now? Why break the pattern?* John thought and thought. Nothing made sense but his mind wouldn't let go. John read the Wolf's note again and studied the words. He read until he knew it off by heart.

Did he know me? Were the deaths of all those people a sign to me? Were they to form a trail… connections? John thought. *Fuck sake, think man… think.*

John was correct, the serious crime unit were the top of the tree, there were several other departments before a case hit John's desk. When it eventually did, you knew it must be bad. Most of the time it was ritual killings or sexual killings. In John's career, he had never had one this bad. The papers loved it; they knew if Miste was on the case it was serious shit.

"Tossers… leeches…" John said sipping at his drink and recalling the reported news on Claire.

The photo of Claire and Carole lay on John's desk, the small newspaper cuttings John had kept from Claire's passing sat spread near his keypad. Claire's wrist bracelet from Carole was placed on the windowsill. John liked the way the sun hit it in the mornings and it gave a golden glow round the room. Claire's

135

wedding ring was in John's hand, he turned and twisted it in his fingers at the same speed as his thoughts. He was allowed to keep these items; once forensics had done their works, John grabbed them back.

"Don't forget about me!" a voice said in the room.

"I want justice!" said the voice again.

John sat back in his chair, his eyes closed and his hands on his face. Claire's ring dropped to the floor.

"Yes, yes, I know… I'm trying… What more can I do? Jesus," John said, his voice filling the small room.

Carole stood in the door opening on the landing. She was naked with only the chain on her neck. Her hair was stringy and untidy to the side of her head. No signs of the trauma she suffered but a look of gloom on her face. The image was solid and the light from the room lit her skin a golden yellow, her eyes glaring at John and not blinking. John looked several times, like a child looking around the corner of a wall in a playground. He didn't stare as the images haunted him. John grabbed the small glass and swung his chair round with a thump. He threw his glass towards Carole…

"What fucking more can I do? If you lot gave me something to work with I could probably catch the bastard," John said as the glass smashed against the stair banister. The glass fragments covered the carpet.

Carole was gone.

"Shit… shit… Now look… shit…" John said swinging his chair back round to the computer and the monitor lighting up his face. John took a deep breath and glared at the screen, his beating heart calming and settling and the image of Carole passing through his mind. The room was silent. Only the light from John's inbox shined up at his face. John blinked trying to wake his heavy eyes.

"Emails… forgot about the emails, John," he said to himself.

John put his hand on the mouse and hovered over his inbox,

he clicked, and the email from Wren earlier sat glaring at him, the title 'Light reading, Boss' clear on the message. This made John smile.

John stared at the email; he read every word twice, blinking deeply. The words bounced round the corners of his mind.

"It can't be, it's impossible," John said out loud.

The results on John's computer screen were clear, nothing had ever been clearer.

DNA matched to records, John Miste... site contamination report issued.

John slowly sat back into his chair, he pulled his glass closer and refilled it from the whisky bottle beside him. He gripped the glass and drank the contents in one gulp, the words he had just read running in his mind. He fiddled with the pen on his desk turning it round and round, counting in his mind.

John was always careful, he always made sure he took the necessary precautions. It was a ritual to John; his OCD wouldn't allow anything less. John racked his mind going through every detail, following the case step by step in his mind. He knew he was clear. He knew he had been the normal John that covered his arse!

"I was careful, I know I was careful... this doesn't make sense!" John said again, the glass still tightly held in his right hand.

John picked up his mobile phone and called Wren.

"Wren... Wren, it's John... I... had to call someone," John said.

"Sir, it's 1 am. What's... what... what's wrong?" Wren said, wiping the sleep from her eyes and trying to recover from the shock of being woken so abruptly.

"Sorry to call you so late, I lost track of time... I didn't know who else to call," John said, still glaring at the screen as if taking in a silent movie...

"What's wrong? Has something happened?" Wren said

lifting herself from her bed and swinging herself out of the covers.

"The email you sent me earlier from Jacob... did you read it?" John asked.

"No... no... didn't get a chance, just forwarded it straight to you... why?" Wren said.

"The DNA results, there... well... they... " John stumbled. "It's my DNA!" John said.

"That's impossible, sir, must be an error!" said Wren.

"It's 99.9%, Wren. Fucking hell... it couldn't be clearer!" John said, sitting back in his chair.

"It's got to be some sort of contamination, I wouldn't worry. Our DNA is on the system to rule us out!" Wren said, her eyes beginning to close again after the shock waking.

"I know that, you daft sod... it's not mine, Wren!" said John.

"You're confusing me, sir. You said it's your DNA... perhaps it's because I'm tired and you woke me up!" said Wren in a sarcastic manner.

"I know what I said, Wren, but it's not mine... but the DNA matches my profile. Something is amiss here!" said John, putting his glass down, his fingers white from the grip where he had held it tightly.

"Sir, get some rest. We can get on to this in the morning," Wren said, lying back on to the bed with the phone pressed against her ear.

"Yes... yes... you're right... yes... better with a clear head... goodnight, Wren," John said, hanging up the phone.

The light from the street lamp was glaring through John's window, the rain heavier and a sense of darkness filled the air. The faces of all the victims stuck to John's wall leapt out at him as if they had a life of their own. John felt their pain.

"Something is seriously wrong here. Claire, what the hell is going on?" John said out loud.

22

The next morning was a clear, bright day, the sun was high in the sky and the smell of the fresh air from the night before tickled at your nose. The wet paths and roads shone in the sun. It was 7 am and John had already left his home. He didn't get much sleep at all, the images, the evidence jumping through his mind. John couldn't figure out what this all meant. John sat on the small brown bench in his local park overlooking the green. He sat here many times to think. The chewing gum went round and round his mouth. It gave him a sense of peace. John and Claire spent many an afternoon there just walking and talking. It made you feel away from it all, a peace that you can only get from those sorts of places. The trees seemed to shield the space, standing tall against the park railings. It reminded John of the woods and lake from when he was a child. The water on the grass glistened and the sound of the early morning bird calls filled the air. A distant milk van could be heard clattering down the side streets, stopping and starting with that familiar sound of a battery as it forces itself into life after a cold night.

John looked tired. His coat was wrapped up tight as there was a chill in the air. He sat back on the bench, hands behind his head, thinking and contemplating, the images of what he had seen the last few days playing through his mind. He knew this was too much of a coincidence to not be anything.

His detective mind went over every detail. All the deaths, the evidence they had, what it all meant.

At that point, John's phone rang loud in his pocket, jumping him from his deep thought.

"Wren... Bleeding hell..." John said.

"Sir, you sound like shit," said Wren.

"Didn't get much sleep; was up all night trying to tie this shit together," John said, rubbing at his stubble.

"It's a mistake, sir, must be," Wren said.

"Do me a favour; until we know what is going on here, keep this under wraps, please. Can you do that for me, Wren?" John asked in a calm voice.

There was a pause as Wren took in what John had said.

"Yes, sir, for now... but we will be asked. You know that," said Wren.

"I know, but for now, let's sit on it until I can think straight," said John.

"Okay... understood. The reason I called is that we have the boyfriend, Nathan; picked up by a marked car," said Wren.

"And the van," said John, Wren's words alive like electricity in John's mind.

"Yes, sir, we have the van that matches the witness statements, and the photo from Carole's room" said Wren.

John took a breath and closed his eyes. Wren's words were like a lottery win to John. Could this be the end of all the shit, all the comments from his superiors and the shit he faced from the papers?

"Fantastic, I'll meet you at the office. Don't talk to him until I'm there," said John, lifting himself from the bench and his chewing gum still going round his mouth.

"Okay, sir," said Wren.

John had left his house earlier in a daze, he had taken his pill just before he left and grabbed an apple. His hair was a mess and his face said it all. He looked like a man who had been out partying all night and had come straight to work without any sleep. John had been up all night but it wasn't a party. He just couldn't get the email out of his mind. He had asked Claire to help but the room was silent. John had never felt so alone. Did they know something he didn't? Had they left him? John's mind was ablaze with thoughts. John left the park and walked to the bus stop at the top of a nearby road. It had a bin fixed to the pole that was still smouldering from the night before. It looked like it had been melted in two. The smell of burning plastic hung in the air. The bus sign was so badly covered in graffiti that you could only just see the name of the stop.

"Fucking mess... haven't they got anything better to do?" John said as he looked at the sight in front of him. It must have been on fire a while and even put itself out as the pole for the bus sign, once silver, was now black and stained.

John stood at the stop and got out his ID badge; he placed the chewing gum back in its silver wrapper and looked at his ID badge. He stared at his picture and the words 'Detective Inspector'. He felt unworthy of this.

The sound of the large engine rumbled up to John and the bus stopped.

"Leicester Police Station," John said and the bus left. John knew this bus took him to the station but he also knew it wasn't a straight journey. It gave John time to think and contemplate his next move.

Nathan arrived at the police headquarters at 9 am, his image exactly as per the photo on Carole's dresser, but not as Mr Peters described. He didn't look the type to be associated with Carole. His clothes were dirty and dated, he wore a black leather jacket with Harley Davidson on the back and his hair was short and flat to his head. He was thin and gaunt. His eyes seemed to stare through you rather than at you. He looked like he hadn't slept for days and the smell around him was alcohol and drugs. His hands were cuffed behind his and

141

pale skin and bony arms stood out against the silver cuffs on his wrists.

The reception at HQ was like any other police station; the main reception desk stood tall and faced you as soon as you walked in, the CCTV cameras pointing and watching at every angle. Behind the desks were the cells and just past them were the interview rooms. Nathan was twitchy as soon as he arrived. The two officers that brought him in spotted him by chance parked in a lay-by. They were not even sure at that stage if the van was occupied. The shock of two police officers knocking on the blackened camper windows would be enough to shock anyone. Nathan didn't open the camper doors, the officers tried the door and it was open. Nathan was slumped on the small couch inside the camper and had been smoking weed. The aroma in the air was strong. The small 12v light gave a low yellow glow, just enough to make out Nathan. There was a small kitchen and burner and a few small cupboards. The curtain had been pulled tight covering the front driver's seat. It was a standard camper inside and Nathan hadn't changed a thing. Apart from the smell of the weed, the interior and exterior was very clean and tidy.

Nathan put up a small struggle but he was that stoned he couldn't hold off the two officers. They soon had him cuffed and slumped against the camper window.

The lay-by was buzzing with SOCO; forensics were all over the camper checking every detail. Wren had made sure the camper wasn't moved and the forensic team had the best chance at getting the evidence they needed. The police presence was large. Chloe had arranged for any DNA traces to be sent straight to Jacob. Wren was clear to the team that as far as they were aware Carole could have been in there and they were to check every detail. The smallest drop of blood could break the case.

Nathan was twitching and beginning to wake from his drugged state. He stretched his neck and rubbed at his eyes, he gave out a large yawn and began to speak.

"Why am I here? What the hell is going on?" he said, resting his cuffed hands on the counter.

"You have been apprehended by the two officers for questioning relating to a murder enquiry," said the charging sergeant behind the counter.

"Have you been read your rights?" said the charging officer again.

"Fucking joke this is… fucking joke. I was minding my own business, wasn't harming anyone… fucking joke," Nathan said banging the counter.

"Have the two officers read you your rights?" he said.

"Yes, they have said some bullshit," said Nathan in a raised voice.

"He was found in his camper in possession of a class B drug," said the officers and Nathan butted in with. "That's for personal use, not for any other fucker."

"As I was saying, Sergeant, he was found in possession and his vehicle matches the witness' description," said the officer.

"What are you talking about? What witness, what vehicle?" said Nathan.

The sergeant went through the processes of booking Nathan in. They took his fingerprints and his DNA. The file for Nathan had now begun. They had checked the system and he had no previous history.

23

John arrived at the office at 11 am. He had taken the long way round on the bus to clear his mind. It gave him a chance to go over every detail part by part. He walked in and went straight to his office, grabbing a tea from the canteen and a small breakfast bar from the vending machine near their office. Mary had seen him briefly and they exchanged a few words about the meal the other night. She told John he looked like shit which reminded him why he had kept himself away from any mirrors that morning. The office was buzzing; they now had two vehicles being checked, Carole's and Nathan's and they had Nathan in custody. This was good progression for the Wolf case.

Wren had been asked for the DNA results by the DCI earlier but she covered for John and said they hadn't received them from Jacob. Lying was hard for Wren; if there was one thing you could say about Wren, it was that she was no liar.

"Sir, where the hell have you been? I've had the DCI all over me and I've covered for you," said Wren to John as he walked into the office chewing on the breakfast bar.

"The bus was delayed. Thanks for covering... I'll sort all this out... just need time to understand what the hell is going on," said John, pulling Wren to one side so they could speak quietly.

"Sir, we won't have long to hold this back, so whatever

you're thinking… think fast," said Wren, handing John the file on Nathan. "He is checked in and we need to act on him," said Wren.

"Okay, let's get in there and see what he knows," said John, still chewing his breakfast bar.

"Sir, Carole's car, the results are back," said Clive, looking at his screen.

"And?" said John walking over to Clive's desk.

"There are blood traces in the car, we are checking our file now," said Clive.

"Blood traces, where?" said John.

"In the boot. Rest of the car was clean… yes, very clean," said Clive.

"What do you mean, very clean?" asked John.

"I would say, and according to forensics, it was cleaned professionally," said Clive, looking deeply at his screen.

"Cover up?" said John.

"Or perhaps a valet?" said Wren. "She was a tidy lass, you could tell that from her home and upbringing."

"It's more than that," said Clive "We are talking full-blown bleach down," said Clive.

"Okay, okay, good work, Clive. What the hell would they be covering with a clean like that? More blood…? Murder?" said John.

"Let me know when the DNA on the blood comes through," said John. "Chloe, how did you do on the jeweller?" John said.

"I checked with them and they have no record. Checked CCTV and it only goes back two weeks so nothing on there," said Chloe.

"Fuck, another dead end… Okay, good work, guys, keep digging. There has got to be something," said John, tapping at the table near Clive's computer.

"There was one thing, sir, one thing that he mentioned," said Chloe just as Wren and John had begun to head away.

"Jesus, Chloe, spit it out, will you?" John said, standing at the door, his coat unzipped now, revealing a black shirt and white buttons.

"He mentioned a guy coming in probably one week after the bracelets were purchased asking about them. He says he remembers him because he drove a distinct vehicle that he parked outside the shop," said Chloe.

"Distinct vehicle? Let me guess… camper van?" said John in a sarcastic manner.

"That's the one, sir. He said the guy who came in was wearing a black jacket, very handsome chap, dark hair. And boots. He said he was very polite and asked if he knew who had purchased the bracelets. They had been in the window for a while before Carole and Claire bought them.

"He said he was hoping to buy them for his daughters," Chloe said, reading the info from her small notepad she took with her to sites.

"That description doesn't sound like our man downstairs," said John. "Unless our shop owner didn't have his glasses on!"

"It does however sound like the description Mr Peters gave us earlier!" John said.

"Nothing on CCTV?" Wren asked.

"Nothing. He is old school and just records over old footage," said Chloe.

"Okay, okay, let's not get too excited with this, let's keep it in mind and see if we can use it downstairs," said John. "It may be something or nothing, but it still may be something."

"Let's head down, Wren. Chloe, go and see him again and take a picture of Nathan. The sergeant has him on file now; would be good to see if he matches the description of the man he saw. Take one of the camper as well, be clear and tell him we are investigating a murder and it's important he racks his brain. Anything he might have forgotten!" John said heading out of the office with Wren.

Nathan had been moved from his holding cell and was being escorted into interview room 4. It was bigger than the other rooms and had a mirrored viewing wall. Mary was already positioned in there with a coffee, ready to listen in. It was the first time since the Wolf struck that a suspect had been brought in for questioning; the first time HQ could say they had someone who matched witness testimony.

The red light above the interview room door glowed red and the word 'Occupied' shone brightly. The heavy wood door saying 'Interview Room 4', hung heavy on its hinges. John and Wren walked into the room. Nathan was sitting arms crossed sipping at his coffee. He stared at John and Wren as they walked in. He was in custody clothes as his clothes had been removed previously for evidence. He looked more fed up than earlier and you could tell he was ready for a fight. The on-call solicitor was sitting beside him busying through the file in front of him and bringing himself up to date with the situation. Nathan looked as bad as he felt. The LED lighting in the room glowed bright and the white light bounced off the wooden table and glowed against the walls. The steam from Nathan's coffee filled the air.

John and Wren walked up to the table with an air of certainty. John pulled out his chair and sat himself down, and the file he was holding was placed with in front of him. Wren followed suit. John shuffled in his seat for a while then looked up at Nathan and smiled.

"DI Miste and DS Walker, the time is 11.30 am and we are here to interview Nathan Brown. Interview commencing." As John finished his sentence he pushed the record button on the unit on the desk, and the machine kicked into life.

John opened the file in front of him and shuffled with the paperwork inside. It had been prepared by his team and had everything they had on Nathan. There was nothing of any major significance but they were sure he knew more than he made out.

"You like camper vans then?" John said still looking over the file and not looking up at Nathan.

"What's that supposed to mean?" said Nathan staring at John's head and holding his hot coffee.

"We had one when I was a kid, me and my brother, used to go all over in it. Original model similar to yours but not as posh… Took some grief on that when I was at school," John said, still looking through the file and not raising his head to look at Nathan.

John fiddled in his pocket and pulled out the silver foil he wrapped his gum in earlier; he unfolded it and placed the gum in his mouth.

"John… John… It's not him, John…" a voice said.

The voice broke John from the file and he looked round the room. He looked over Nathan and behind Wren. Everyone looked at him. Wren was looking at John then at Nathan.

"What did you say, Nathan?" asked John, looking at him with glared eyes.

"This boy has lost the plot… You all right there, Detective… Shit… fucking shows why I'm here and you ain't out there catching the bastards plaguing the streets," said Nathan, laughing and taking deep swigs from his coffee.

Behind the mirror, Mary was listening in and taking gentle sips of her coffee, the speaker in the room repeating every word John was asking. It had the level of a train platform speaker and there was a small delay.

This made it difficult sometimes with the words being spoken and the sound. Mary heard John ask the question.

"What the hell are you doing, John?" she said out loud.

"It's Claire, John, it's me… he isn't… it's not…" the voice broke away.

John was looking round the room frantically. He had fallen into his own world and Claire's words were rolling round his mind. He knew what he heard and it was as clear as ever. He looked in all the corners hoping to see her standing there but the room was clear. John was sweating on his brow. He got up from his chair and walked towards the mirror, he stared in the mirror at himself and settled his thoughts with a few deep breaths. On the other side, Mary was looking directly at John and checking his expression.

"Sir," said Wren, breaking John's state.

John shook his head and came back out of his trance.

"I haven't got all day, Detective," said Nathan in a sarcastic manner.

"Campers, do you like camper vans?" John asked again as he stood with his back to the mirror and his hands crossed in front of him. His large frame cast an imposing shadow onto the table.

"Yes, I like camper vans or I wouldn't bleeding own one, would I?" said Nathan, getting more annoyed by the moment.

"You're a mechanic, right?" said John, walking back to his seat and settling back down into the present situation. "You're a mechanic and you work at Joe's in town; is that correct?" said John looking at his file.

"Yes, that's correct... AND?" said Nathan.

"Have you worked there long?"

There was a pause then Nathan said, "Look, I'm a mechanic. I've worked there ten years, I own a camper van which I bought as a shit heap and spent hours building the fucking thing. I'm not married and I have a girlfriend... ANYTHING ELSE?" said Nathan, clearly fed up with the questioning.

Nathan slumped back in his chair and crossed his arms, he flung his head back and let out a sigh.

"What is this shit about? Is someone going to tell me?" said Nathan.

"See, the problem is, son, there was another murder associated with the our case, but this time we had a witness who saw a camper van," said John.

"So, there are hundreds of camper vans. So fucking what?" said Nathan.

"This van was described in detail, and it's funny, Nathan… well, we think it is… that it had blacked-out windows and shiny wheel trims! Ring a bell?" said John, looking directly at Nathan.

A silence fell over the interview room; only the buzzing of the recorder could be heard and the faint noise of the busy corridor outside.

"I've not done anything wrong, I don't know what the hell you guys are going on about. So I smoked weed, and was stoned… so what? Book me and let me go. Jesus!" said Nathan, throwing his hands into the air.

"Do you know a girl by the name of Carole Peters?" John said, looking down at his notes as if he was reading her name from them. Nathan looked at John and John looked back at him. For a moment, their eyes met, studying each other and looking for the slightest of reactions.

"She is my girl; we are seeing each other. What's that got to do with this?" said Nathan.

"She was found a few nights ago, murdered, and her body was dumped in a park car park. Your van was spotted!" said John, looking at Nathan.

Nathan's head was turning from side to side. It was as if he was looking at a busy road and checking to cross it. Sensing this, John continued: "Where were you four nights ago?" said John studying Nathan's reaction.

There was a silence.

"I'll ask again, where were you four nights ago? Sunday night, if it helps?" John said again.

The acting solicitor leaned over to Nathan and whispered in his ear. John settled back in his chair with his arms crossed, a faint smile on his face. He took the chewing gum out of his mouth and placed it in the ashtray on the table in front of them.

"I didn't fucking do anything. What do you mean, don't say anything? This is bollocks!" Nathan said to his solicitor staring at him with daggers.

"What the hell are you saying? She is dead? No one has told me… this is all bollocks!" said Nathan. "I have tried ringing her for the last few days. We had… well… a small argument… Nothing major, just a bust-up… I can't believe what I'm hearing."

"The type of bust-up that ends in violence, Nathan? Forces you to chop at her body and dump her like she is worth nothing?" said John as he kept pushing.

"Nothing like that at all. She wanted us to go away, fucking break to the seaside, it's not my bag… We had only been seeing each other a few weeks. Her parents hated me," said Nathan.

"What do you mean, hated you? They only met you once at his house!" said Wren.

"What are you on about, I never met them. They just hated me, not right for their daughter, a mechanic. How can they judge without at least meeting me!Her dad made it clear; thought I couldn't hear but I did. 'He is no good for you, Carole, no good… common…' Tosser! Who is he to judge me! Shouted it while she was on the phone to me," said Nathan, waving his hands in the air and jumping from his chair and marching over to the mirror.

John and Wren looked at each other for a moment

"Are you saying you never went to the house?" said John

"That's correct, Detective, well done there… I wasn't welcome!" said Nathan

"Mr Peters was very particular about his daughter, Nathan. She was his special girl, good upbringing, educated," said John looking at Nathan leaning against the mirror with his hands against his face.

"Do you have any hard evidence linking Nathan to the scene, Detective?" said the solicitor to John. "Or are you going to hound him with the family not liking him spiel!"

The fact was, John didn't. Nathan's DNA was not in Carole's car, nor was it on her body. There was no sexual contact to report and nothing at the scene. The only strong evidence was DNA matching John's.

During the interview, the team had been searching Carole's phone and also checking Nathan's. They had recovered voice messages from Nathan apologising for the other night and saying Mr Peters had pissed him off. He wanted to make up. On the night of Carole's murder Nathan's phone was in the mechanic workshop where it didn't move for the rest of the night. Nathan's phone also showed text messages to Carole on that night apologising. Carole's phone didn't reply.

"I can't believe this shit," said Nathan, walking back over to the chair and slumping down in it. His hands were to his face and he was beginning to wipe tears away. John and Wren looked at each other and gave a slight smile.

"Nathan, it's as simple as this: your van matches the description of a van spotted at the scene, the victim was your girlfriend. You had a fight… it's not looking good here… throw us a bone!" said John.

Nathan's hands were still to his face and he was crying.

"I've looked through these notes and I can't see any hard evidence that links my client to this case. Either charge him for possession or let him go," said the solicitor.

"Wait… wait… I remember… four nights ago… ha ha… I remember," said Nathan, leaping to life.

"You don't have to say anything, Nathan," said the solicitor.

John gave the solicitor daggers then looked back at Nathan.

"Okay, Nathan, what?" said John, tapping on the file in front of him.

"I worked late, late on a Merc… it was for one of our regular customers, you see. He, well, he travels and does stupid hours… spends a fortune with us… so our gaffer pays us to work late to get it done. He dropped it 4 pm ish the day before and me and Bert worked on it all night. It was a full sump change, right pain in the arse," said Nathan.

The room was silent. John looked at Nathan and Wren looked at John. Mary put her hands to her face and rubbed her eyes. The sense of a sinking ship fell in John's mind. Nathan had an alibi.

"Speak to Bert; he can verify it," said Nathan.

Wren took Bert's details from Nathan and left the room.

"Okay, so you worked late. Are there any CCTV cameras at your place?"

"I think so, why?" said Nathan.

"Because if you worked late and didn't leave, the camera will also verify this," said John making notes.

"And your camper? Where do you park it?" said John.

"At the back. It's near the other motors and safe," said Nathan.

"Any cameras there?" said John.

"One, I think," said Nathan.

"Look, I've done nothing, mate, fuck all... Speak to Bert, he can tell you; even my gaffer, Mark, he will tell you," said Nathan with his arms crossed and a sense of calm on him.

John sat for a moment and looked at Nathan. He took in the room and you could sense the foreboding had lifted. A police interview room can be a funny thing; you can feel guilty even if you're not. It puts a kind of aura on you, a dark cloud. The cloud had lifted and the weather had changed. Nathan was in the driving seat.

"Interview terminated," John said as he switched off the recorder.

"Can I go now?" said Nathan.

"Yes, you can go but leave your details with the charging sergeant and he will book you for possession. Don't leave the country as we may need to talk again," John said, lifting himself from the chair.

"One more thing," said John, turning to Nathan with one hand on the door.

"When my guys brought you in, you were stoned. Do you smoke until you black out or just small amounts?"

"What?" said Nathan.

"Your smoking; is it to oblivion or paced?" John said again.

"Fifty-fifty… depends what mood I'm in," said Nathan looking at John as if he was a school teacher just preparing to tell him off.

John nodded and you could sense his mind working. He opened the door fully, leaned back against it, and waved at Nathan to go. Nathan walked past John and into the corridor. Nathan stopped and turned to look back at John.

"Should I go and see the family?" said Nathan.

"I wouldn't at the moment; wouldn't be the best thing to do, pal," said John, staring at Nathan. "You were not flavour of the month before this, let alone now," John said.

"What about my van?" said Nathan.

"What?" said John, shutting the interview room door and entering the corridor.

"My van. When can I have that back? I don't have another vehicle," said Nathan again.

"Escort him out," John said to the solicitor standing with Nathan.

"Loved that van more than me… bastard," said a voice behind John.

John turned and it was Carole, as clear as day standing with her hands to her face wiping her eyes, the light of the corridor reflecting off her dress. Her long hair was soft against her shoulders, and the gold necklace sparkled in the light.

"I'm sorry!" John whispered as he looked at her with a tear in his eye.

"John?" said Mary.

John turned on hearing Mary's voice and as he turned back Carole was gone. As quick as she appeared she had vanished.

"John, what the hell was that? Don't we have anything we can charge him on?" said Mary. "What about DNA?" she said.

"Negative, it's not his DNA!" said John.

"Who then?" said Mary.

"We are looking into it still, ma'am," said John walking off towards his office, escaping before Mary dug deeper.

24

It was 6.30 pm before John arrived at the doctors for his monthly check. John sat in the small waiting room looking at a magazine. His phone had rung several times on the way there and John had answered every call. He had instructed Clive to go to the garage where Nathan worked and pull up the CCTV images, and he had asked for the phone reports. The phone reports tied in with Nathan's story. Wren had also spoken to Bert who confirmed Nathan's story. The net was closing. John sat looking at a magazine four years out of date, the yellow lighting above flickering and the pages John was turning not even sinking in his mind. He looked up from his magazine and looked round the waiting room. All the other patients sat doing exactly the same as John, looking at magazines years out of date and not really taking anything in. The magazines were stacked high on the small brown table in the middle of the seating. The people were like robots, the coughing rumbling into the air. John threw the magazine down and rubbed at his eyes. It had been a long day of shit. No further forward now than John had been in the past. Every time they seemed to get closer a brick wall was built. The only key things John had was the camper van and the DNA. John fumbled in his pocket for his gum but he had finished this during the day. He also realised he had only had a small breakfast bar in the morning and hadn't eaten since. *Bleeding hell,* John thought, rubbing at his eyes again.

"John Miste, please," a nurse holding a clipboard called.

John lifted himself up and walked towards the nurse. He could feel the eyes in his back like daggers as John walked towards the mental health room. *I'm mental... watch out... not as mental as the bastards I have to deal with...* John would think, feeling the eyes digging in his back.

John met with his doctor and went through the same old shit; how's life? How's work? Any stresses? Any changes? On and on...

John knew the routine and he didn't have to say much. They were too keen just to write the prescription and send John on his way. Another set of special pills to help him operate.

John was in and out within an hour.

John walked outside the doctors and looked up at the sky. The weather was changing and the sky was dark. John pulled his coat tight and headed to the bus stop. The traffic was getting heavy and the roads were vibrating with the noise of the city traffic rumbling over them. John's phone rang.

"Sir, it's Clive."

"Go ahead, Clive, what's up?" said John.

"We have the CCTV back from the garage. You're going to like this!" said Clive.

"Go ahead," said John as he ran over the road, leaping between oncoming vehicles and doing his best not to fall on his arse.

"We have the camper and we have images of it being taken," said Clive.

"What, stolen?" said John, taking deep breaths as he sat down at the bus stop.

"No, sir, the perpetrator just opened the door and within a few minutes drove away as clear as day."

John paused and took in what Clive was saying.

"Are you saying Nathan's van was taken and returned?"

"Yes, sir, we have it returned clear as day in the early hours; same position, everything, a few hours later," said Clive.

"Do you see the guy's face?" said John.

"No, he is wearing full black attire and gloves," said Clive.

"Do you have Nathan coming out of the garage at any point?" said John.

"We have Nathan leaving the garage at the front and going over to the kebab shop, but he is back in minutes with food. He never goes out the back, sir," said Clive.

John stands and waves at the approaching bus, one hand in the air and the other on his phone pressed tight against his ear.

"Why the hell would you take an old camper, use it for the murder, drop it back… unless…" John paused.

"Unless what, sir?" said Clive.

"'Unless he used Nathan's van to lure her, from a distance she would have thought it was Nathan if he was in the right place at the right time. He could have doen this several times without Nathan knowing. That means it wasn't Nathan at the Peters house, it was the Wolf. That's why the witness statement from the Peters, doesn't match the photo of Nathan! He was checking her out."

The penny had dropped in John's mind, he was beginning to see how much detail and time the Wolf put into his catch. He knew he took his time but to go to this extent, was beyond what John thought. John had to up his game.

25

The team had worked hard piecing together the fragments of information they had, and piecing together the interviews and witness statements. Nothing made sense and it certainly didn't lead to Nathan as he was in the clear. The Wolf was clever and whatever game he was playing he was on top form and well ahead of the police. He seemed to know every step before they did. You could cut the atmosphere with a knife in the office. The tension and frustration was rife in all their minds.

John had arrived home late that evening. It had been a challenging day. By the time he had got off the bus and made his way along the streets to his house, it was 8 pm. Wren had called and asked if he fancied a Chinese. John didn't think much of Chinese food as it gave him gas. He had tried it once with Claire and he spent most of the night being sick with his head over the toilet. It could have been the prawns… who knew? Just the thought made John's stomach gurgle. He did, however, agree and Wren was due at 9 pm. She was also bringing her other half who she had been seeing a while; his name was Michael. John got in and carried out his normal routine, he had a shower and changed his clothes, he took his pill and even managed to clear the front room that was covered in paperwork again. His office was like a memorial wall, the faces of all the victims placed evenly on the wall and the string linking all areas. Maps were crossed and then re-marked, and the small desk lamp was still lit shining at John's desk from the night before. The email from Wren and the DNA results were still clear in John's mind; he knew he had to come out with the truth but he also knew he would be taken off the case pending an enquiry. This was too close for John and he wasn't having any of it.

I just need time to sort this... time to figure this out, he thought as he dried himself from the hot shower.

The steam was filling the bathroom and the small Victorian window struggled with the level of steam it was being asked to remove. John stood in front of the mirror and wiped away the condensation, he looked at himself and wiped at his face. He thought how old he looked and he felt the pressure building on his shoulders.

The strain on his face was as clear as day, the results tumbling through his mind.

Wren and Michael were on their way. Wren had picked Michael up from his home just outside Leicester in a small village called Kilby. It was an old farm house up a long country drive. She had picked up the food and was heading to John's. Wren had been seeing Michael for a while now. Wren wasn't the sort to discuss her love life at work and she liked to keep this separate so even John didn't know the full details. Michael wasn't living with Wren and he had his own place that backed on to woodland. He worked away a lot and they didn't get much time to spend together, but Wren knew she loved him. He treated her better than any other man had and she still, had to pinch herself on how she landed him. Michael was a tall, good-looking man, early forties, much older than Wren, but he looked in his early thirties. He worked in construction and had done all his life. He had the look of a well-travelled man and a smile you could die for. He always dressed very tidily and seemed to look good in whatever he wore. Wren was in awe of him. They had met while out in the town and he had approached Wren, he treated her well and had the softest of touches. If you looked at them they didn't seem to match, but somehow it worked.

Wren's Audi pulled onto John's street. There were only a few spaces left as all the residents were at home. The light from the street lamps glowed against the trees lining the road. It was a clear, cool evening. The windows along the houses all glowed from the lights behind, and the peace that only a street can have at this time of night, filled the air. Wren and Michael left the car and Wren struggled with the lock for a while until it jumped into life and gave a flash of the indicators.

"You need to get that sorted, sweetie," said Michael, standing on the path and adjusting his suit jacket.

"I know... John keeps saying the same... it's just been manic at work, you know, with the case and things," said Wren.

A police rule – you don't discuss your work with anyone outside the force, but love, well, it's a strange thing. It can make you weak and your most secret of thoughts can escape during a meal or a drink. Wren and Michael had had numerous conversations about Wren's work

Michael was always willing to listen and would take in all the details.

Although he didn't discuss much of his work with Wren, he always told her he didn't find his job stressful, not like hers.

Wren and Michael pressed John's doorbell, the light from inside John's house lighting up Wren and Michael through the Victorian stained glass, the colours bouncing off their clothes. John made his way down the stairs. He was wearing a pair of blue jeans and a black shirt tucked in. He had tidied his hair and looked presentable. John didn't like entertaining, it was always Claire's thing, but the doctors always told him it helped so he tried his best.

"Wren, come on in," John said as he opened the front door with a smile on his face. "You must be Michael; I would like to say I've heard a lot about you but she doesn't let much out," John said, extending his hand to shake Michael's hand.

Michael took John's hand and shook it. His handshake was firm, that of a builder, but his skin was soft.

"Good to meet you too, John, Wren has told me a lot about you... All good, don't worry!" said Michael with a smile on his face.

John waved them both in and they made their way into the front room, John closed the door and headed into the kitchen. Wren followed with the bag of Chinese food at her side. John had tidied well, in fact better than Wren had seen in a while. The kitchen was spotless and looked bright and airy. It was as if Claire was back and had been busy cleaning.

"You've been busy; you didn't have to go to this trouble!" Wren said in a quiet voice as she placed the food on the counter.

"I wanted to make an effort for your guy... don't want him thinking I'm a slob!" said John, smiling gently and opening the fridge to reveal some cold beers he had picked up on his way home.

"Michael, would you like a beer? They are cold... bought them myself!" said John picking up one of the bottles and aiming it in Michael's direction.

Michael was in the front room standing looking at the photos on the fireplace. There were pictures of John and Claire and a picture of John and Mark. He was studying them and looking closely. His hands were in his pockets and you could see the concentration on his face.

"Michael, beer?" John said again.

"Sorry... Yes, please. I was taken by your photos. You can sense the love jumping from the frame," said Michael, picking up the photo of John and Claire.

John walked over with the beer in his hands, the quiet sound of the radio playing in the background.

"That's Claire, my wife; had a heart of gold... taken from me... Tragic," said John, handing Michael the beer.

"She worked in a school, didn't she?" said Michael, holding the photo in one hand and the beer in the other.

John looked at Michael and then looked at Wren, who was standing in the kitchen dishing out the Chinese on to different plates. She shrugged her shoulders as if to say 'not me'.

"That's right. How do you know that?" said John, taking the photo from Michael's hands and sitting it back on the shelf.

"I'm sorry, don't mean to pry... it was on the news. I remember hearing it, in the papers and all that... the Wolf fellow..." said Michael, sipping at his beer.

"Right, yes... it was indeed," said John.

"Food is ready," Wren said, walking into the room with the plates balanced on her arms and trying to avoid John's small table.

John didn't have a dining table although he was going to get one. When Claire passed away it seemed to slip from his mind.

"Sorry, Michael, I don't have a table: it's a knee job, I'm afraid," said John pointing Michael to the sofa.

"That's fine by me; wouldn't have it any other way," said Michael, sitting down next to Wren on John's sofa.

John settled in the small chair next to the fireplace. He had the fire going and the small lamp next to it lit. The radio played in the background and the environment felt calm.

An awkward silence fell over the room. John picked at the food and put chunks into his mouth.

"How is it?" said Wren.

"Fantastic, lovely," said John, trying his best not to spit out the food.

Wren knew he was lying, but she was happy he was making the effort. She was also happy they could give John some company so he didn't have to spend the evening alone.

"So, Michael, what do you do for a living? Wren mentioned you travel a fair bit," said John, trying to break the ice.

"Yes, that's right, I'm in construction; more site management so I can be here, there and everywhere. We have got sites all over the place at the moment," said Michael, chewing his food and wiping at his mouth as he spoke trying not to spit it all over John.

"Large works?" said John.

"Huge civil fit outs," said Michael.

John nodded in agreement.

"Nothing compared to what you and Wren do. Jesus, I couldn't do it. All that crap with the Wolf thing… it's been all over the papers. How do you deal with that?" said Michael, looking at John.

John paused from eating for a moment and wiped at his mouth with a tissue.

"You have to deal with it… close your mind… if you don't, it can drive you insane," said John.

"Yes, but your wife and everything; I wouldn't be able to cope with that," said Michael, picking up his beer and drinking the last sip.

The room fell quiet and John stared at Michael. John wasn't the best with being questioned, even at work, and he certainly didn't like being questioned in his own home. Wren could sense this and jumped in; "Anyone fancy another drink?" she said, lifting herself from the sofa and heading to John's fridge. John hadn't answered yet and was still taking in Michael's question.

"Have you caught anyone yet?" said Michael.

"Michael, I would rather not talk about the case. It's not something we are supposed to do and not something I want to do. Let's close that door," said John, finishing his beer and staring deeply at Michael.

Michael sensed John's frustration and it seemed to please him, a rife smile lifted onto his face and he slowly continued to eat his Chinese. He had stopped looking at John but John looked deeply at him, taking in all the detail. John looked over at Wren and she was looking stressed. She was hastily trying to open the beer bottles and get back to the scene before John and Michael clashed horns.

"Do you mind if I use your toilet?" said Michael, placing his food on John's small table.

"No, not at all. Top of the stairs, along the corridor and second door on the left," said John.

Michael lifted himself up and adjusting his suit jacket he walked slowly up the stairs towards the bathroom.

"Sorry, John, I thought it was a good idea. You know, give you someone to talk to," said Wren, placing the beers on the small table and slumping down on the sofa with a sigh. John looked at her and smiled.

"It's okay, Wren, don't worry... It's not your fault. He is a nice guy, straight talking like me, but that's not a bad thing," said John, picking up the beer and placing the empty plate on the small table.

26

Definition of a wolf:

A predator; stalks its prey, is patient and works intelligently. Prepared to wait the long wait until it has the prey in its sights. Once the scene is set it attacks. Precise, planned movements, nothing by chance.
DI John Miste

Michael headed up John's stairs. He walked slowly up the small Victorian staircase clinging to the wooden banister and its oak-top finish. He took in the scene in front of him and all the photos on the walls. The moonlight shone brightly through the Victorian stained glass on the loft hatch casting a beautiful, colourful glow over the stairs. The small lamp on the landing gave a soft glow. As Michael got to the top of the stairs, he stopped and looked deeply at the photos on the wall: John and Claire smiling and happy, John's parents with two young boys side by side. The images played in Michael's mind. He adjusted the end photo that still hung crookedly and made his way down the corridor. The toilet came into Michael's view just as John said, but Michael headed to the spare bedroom door. The noise of John and Wren talking downstairs could be heard faintly in the background. The corridor floorboards creaked under Michael's feet.

John's office door was closed; he didn't like leaving this open as the images from the victims seemed to follow him around the house. Michael grabbed hold of the large black Victorian handle and with a small push opened the door. He looked over his shoulder at the stairs to check he was still alone. He was. Michael walked into John's office.

The blinds were open and the light from the street lamp flooded in. John's desk sat covered in paperwork and his desk lamp was still on. An empty whisky bottle sat next to his keyboard.

Michael walked into the room and took in the scene. He pulled a set of black gloves from his pocket and slowly started to pull them over his large hands. He unbuttoned his jacket and made himself feel more comfortable. Michael looked at John's wall, the faces of all the victims, the evidence, the map, all looking back at him. Michael headed over to the wall and smiled.

"Fucking fool... idiot!" he said in a quiet tone, looking closely at the images and his eyes narrowing, focusing on the detail. He read the information on the Wolf and he studied the pictures. He rubbed his gloved left hand against the faces of each victim, but stopped at Claire's...

"You were the hardest, my dear... you were the hardest," he said, rubbing his thumb on Claire's image and smiling as he did. Michael spotted the note from the Wolf, the original note that should have been in evidence, pinned to John's board.

"Now, now, Miste... naughty boy," he said, pulling the note from its pins and placing it in his pocket.

Just at that moment, a shadow fell over the room. John was standing in the doorway looking in at Michael. Michael had been a few minutes by now and John hadn't heard the normal sound of his bathroom door shutting; it had a sound that only John knew. It was something he meant to fix but never got around to it. You had to slam the door to shut it and John hadn't heard that.

"Michael, what are you doing in here? This stuff doesn't concern you," John said, looking in at Michael.

Michael stood in front of the evidence wall, he moved his hands to behind his back and clasped them.

"What are you doing in here?" John said with authority.

Michael smiled and let out a small laugh.

"You know, John, me and you are more alike than you know... more alike than you know. All this shit you have on the wall... yet no nearer to catching the bastard," said Michael, looking at the wall and not once looking over at John.

John looked around the room taking in the scene. His detective mind knew something was wrong; he knew the moment Michael asked him the questions downstairs. He had a gut feeling that something wasn't right. *Why now? Why meet me now after all this time?* During all the time he had been with Wren, not once had he agreed to come round. John sensed this was different. Questions rattled through his mind but the thought of Claire telling him to chill out and stop looking at everyone like a criminal rang in his mind.

John slowly began to walk over to Michael, scanning the room for anything he could grab just in case he needed it. There was nothing; only the empty whisky bottle on John's desk stood a chance. John knew the distance wouldn't work. It was amazing how your mind jumped around when you were faced with these situations. *I'm jumping to conclusions... he just went in the wrong door... he is inquisitive, that's all...* John's mind tossed and turned. The only thing John could grab was a paper clip on his table. He quickly grabbed this and for some unknown reason, tucked it down his trousers.

"Come look at this, John," Michael said, pointing at one of the photos.

John walked into the room and up to Michael. Michael turned and smiled at John. The smile sent a shiver down John's spine. He had seen smiles like this before.

"See this... Claire... how you coped, I don't know," Michael said, tapping at Claire's photo as John looked on.

John was looking at Michael's black gloves as he tapped at the photo. He looked at his face that held a slight smile... not a smile of peace; it was more than that. *Why gloves? You're in my house... they were not on downstairs.*

John had seen these types of smiles before; the bastards he dealt with, you saw the signs. John fiddled silently in his pocket but had nothing he could grab; the room was so quiet. The faint noise of cars rushing by and a dog barking could be heard in the distance. The lamp on John's desk glowed against Michael's face.

"You see, Miste, I thought this would break you... but you're a determined fucker, I'll give you that," said Michael, turning and smiling at John again.

At that point, Wren shouted up the stairs.

"What you guys doing up there? I'll send a search party in a minute," she said joking, looking up the stairs and holding the beer bottle in her hand.

The sound of Wren shouting made John turn. As he did, Michael's hand covered John's mouth. The smell was potent. It wasn't even a second and John drifted slowly to the floor, his body sliding down Michael's legs. John didn't even have a chance to put up a fight; whatever Michael had used was so fast acting it took John out in an instant. The only memory John held was the smell before his mind closed down. Michael let John's body slump down and looked out at the corridor.

"Be one minute, babe, me and John are having a man to man," shouted Michael, moving John's body into a more comfortable position. Michael was careful with John, he handled him not as a victim, but as a small child. He was soft and handled with care. Not normal in these circumstances.

"There, there, big man... soon be over and you can be with your wife," said Michael in a calm and quiet voice.

The room seemed to fall dark for that moment; the silence

and the fear could almost be picked from the air. The pain and agony and the faces from the victims all darkened the scene. The yellow glow from John's desk lamp glowed in the background.

Michael took John by the arms and pulled him into the corridor, the rug in John's office drawing up as his large body dragged along. The light from the moon lit up John's torso, his right slipper had been left in the middle of his office and his arms hung loose. If he wasn't being pulled by Michael, you would have thought John was asleep. Once Michael had pulled John into the corridor he went back into John's office and tidied the scene. He pulled the carpet straight, switched off the desk lamp and settled the scene.

He looked round the room and surveyed the scene. It was quiet and calm, the only sound in the air was the sound of the radio downstairs. Michael held on to the door handle and slowly and quietly pulled John's office door closed. A deep calm was about him and his smile filled his face. There was no rush, no anticipation; pure calm…

There was one thing that was certain; Michael had been clever and smart. He had calculated his every move and planned the act. There was only one more loose end. He knelt down beside John and adjusted his black gloves, pulling them tightly on his hands. He moved John's hands and placed them on his side leaving John in an almost asleep pose. Michael stood and straightened his attire.

"Hey babe, John wants to show you something… come on up," shouted Michael, still looking down at John and smiling at his prize.

"Okay… okay. You boys!" said Wren, placing her beer bottle gently onto the table and wiping her mouth, removing the last deposits of the food. She lifted herself up and headed to the stairs. It was dark but she could hear what she thought were John and Michael on the corridor, the sound of the floorboards dancing in the air.

As she climbed the stairs, the light from the loft window lit her face, the moonlight so bright in the sky that the colours from the old Victorian stained glass shone bright over Wren's body. She finally reached the top of the stairs and looked down the dimly lit corridor. She could see John on the floor and Michael was leaning against the wall with his arms crossed.

"John, what the hell?" said Wren, running down the corridor towards him.

Wren ran towards John and knelt down beside him. She quickly checked his pulse and established he was breathing and looked deeply at his face.

"What happened?" she said, turning and looking at Michael who was still leaning against the wall with his arms crossed and looking down at Wren with a smile on his face.

"Michael, what the hell has happened?" she said again in louder tone, lifting herself from the floor and standing in front of Michael with a concerned look on her face.

Michael took a deep breath.

"It's like a picture, isn't it?" said Michael, opening his eyes and looking down the corridor.

"What the hell are you talking about? What happened to John? He needs help," said Wren who was getting more concerned by the moment. She knelt back down, checking John again and patting at his face for signs of life.

"John… John, for God's sake, John, wake up," said Wren, patting as hard as she could and shaking John's body.

Michael knelt down quickly and grabbed hold of Wren's hair sharply. He put a knife to her neck that he had pulled from his inside jacket pocket. The knife was pressed against Wren's tiny neck, its long silver blade glowing against the coloured light. The blade was clean and long. It had been shone to perfection and the reflection was clear; the reflection of pain…Wren's face clear in the knife's image.

"Michael… No, please, what are you doing? Fuck sake, no,"

said Wren in a distressed tone and still kneeling near John, keeping her hands spread out wide.

"There, there, babe. Look, John is just resting, look at the way the light covers the landing… look, it almost looks like a blood-red moon. How right for this occasion," Michael said, laughing and using the knife to turn Wren's head so she could see down the corridor.

"Please, Michael, what do you want?" said Wren with her head turned and the knife digging deeply into her skin. She balanced with her hands as Michael used the blade to lift her head.

"I've been waiting for this for a long time… a very long time… My word… can't believe it's finally here… just one more loose end… one more…" said Michael closing his eyes.

As he did so, he moved the knife from Wren's throat and plunged it into her back. Wren gave out a cry and Michael covered her mouth with his spare hand in a flash.

"You see, bitch, I've got what I wanted. All I ever wanted was him. John and I are going to have some fun…"

Wren slid to the floor and slumped over John. She was coughing and struggling to breathe. The red light glowed against her body and the shadow of Michael standing over her blackened her face.

"Who… who… are you?" said Wren, struggling to talk as the pain in her body took hold.

Michael leaned down to Wren and pointed the knife at her chest. He moved it up and down her body as if planning where to cut a cake.

"Why, Wren… I'm the Wolf," Michael said plunging the knife again into Wren's chest. His hand again covering her tiny mouth.

The Wolf pressed down on the blade with all his weight, he pressed and turned the knife just to be sure. The blood from Wren's body poured out of her, and the carpet on John's landing turned red. The area fell silent. Wren's body fell silent and her eyes stayed still. Her small hands fell to the side and her mouth hung open. A single tear sat softly on her face. The life and the love had left her body. Her last image and the last sound was Michael... becoming the thing she had hunted for so long... *the Wolf*... Her last image, she took to the grave.

He pulled the knife out of Wren's body, stood up and took a deep breath, he wiped the blade with a hanky he had in his pocket, and put the blade carefully back in his jacket. He placed the bloodstained hanky in Wren's pocket, pushing it in tightly, and gave her a kiss on her cheek.

"Well, that's that... tidy. Just me and you now, John... just me and you."

The Wolf kicked Wren's body and pushed her with his feet so she lay beside John. She was discarded like a rag doll of no purpose. Her face was pressed against the carpet and the blood covered her body. The Wolf took hold of John's body and started dragging him towards the stairs. The red light from the loft hatch lit up the landing, and the horror on the corridor was clear.

The Wolf had planned and predicted; he had manipulated, and Wren, unknowingly, had led him to his prize. Wren had been played. She loved Michael and was happy, she followed her heart and the good nature in her. The love she felt for Michael had drained away, just like her blood leaving her tiny body.

"This is just the beginning, Miste, just the beginning," said the Wolf.

In the darkness of the corridor, a small shadow could be seen; it was Claire. She stood with her hands against her mouth looking at the scene in front of her. The tears streamed down her face and you could feel the pain. She watched the Wolf drag her man down the corridor. The corridor down which they had once both walked hand in hand together, and the corridor that held such fond memories for her, had turned to dark. The light had left the space and only pain remained. The calming energy that surrounded Claire had evaporated into the dark space.

"My John... No, not John," she said in horror.

TO BE CONTINUED...